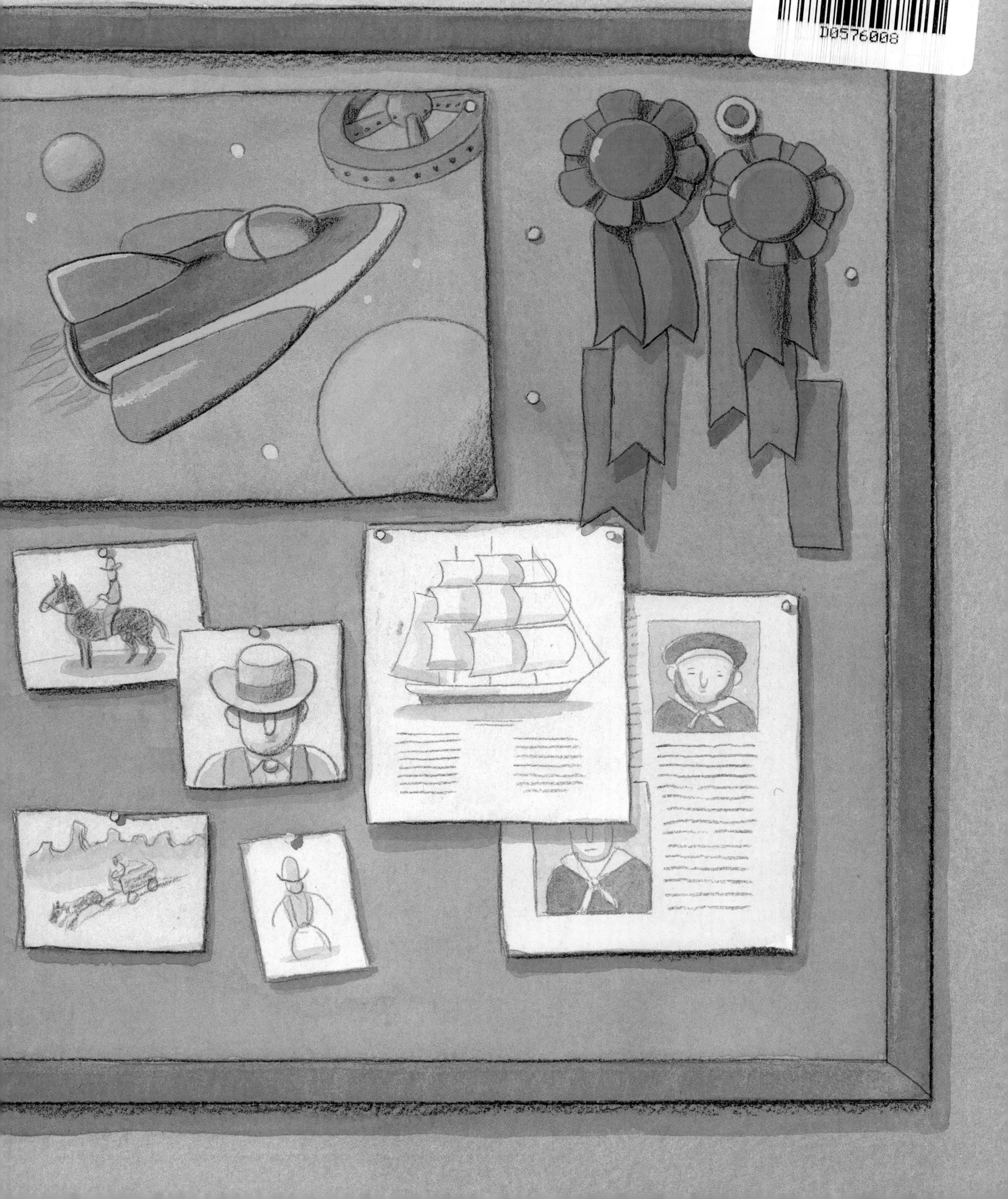

In memory of
Jeff Brown and all
that he has inspired.
Scott

Flat Stanley
Text copyright © 2006 by Jeff Brown
Illustrations copyright © 2006 by Scott Nash

All rights reserved. No part of this book may be used or
reproduced in any manner whatsoever without written
permission except in the case of brief quotations
embodied in critical articles and reviews. For information
address HarperCollins Children's Books, a division of
HarperCollins Publishers, 1350 Avenue of the Americas,
New York, NY 10019.
www.harpercollinschildrens.com

Based on the original *Flat Stanley* by Jeff Brown,
text copyright © 1964.

Library of Congress Cataloging-in-Publication
Data is available.
ISBN-10: 0-06-112904-6
ISBN-13: 978-0-06-112904-9

Printed in the U.S.A.

4 5 6 7 8 9 10

First Edition

# FLAT STANLEY

by Jeff Brown

illustrated by Scott Nash

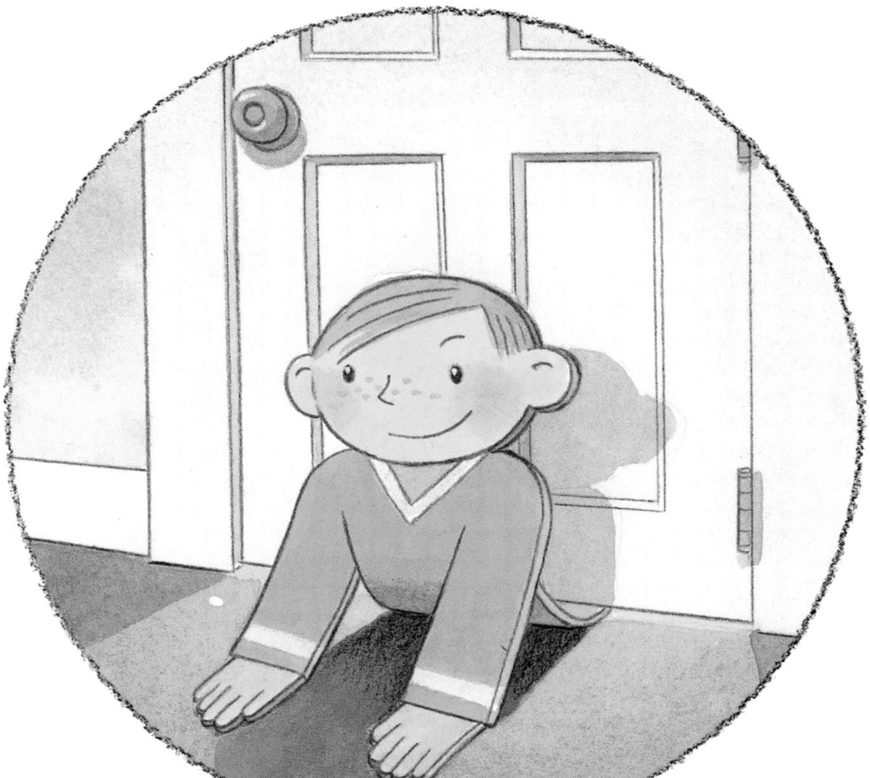

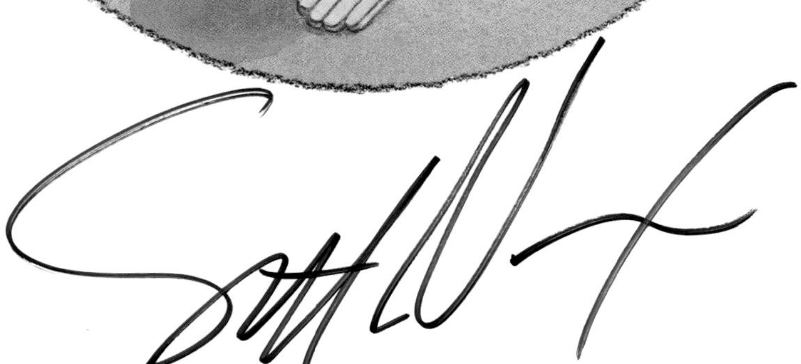

HarperCollinsPublishers

"Hey! Come and look!" Arthur Lambchop called from the
bedroom he shared with his brother, Stanley.
Mr. and Mrs. Lambchop cared greatly for politeness and correct speech.
"Hay is for horses, Arthur, not people," said Mrs. Lambchop.
"But look!" said Arthur, pointing.

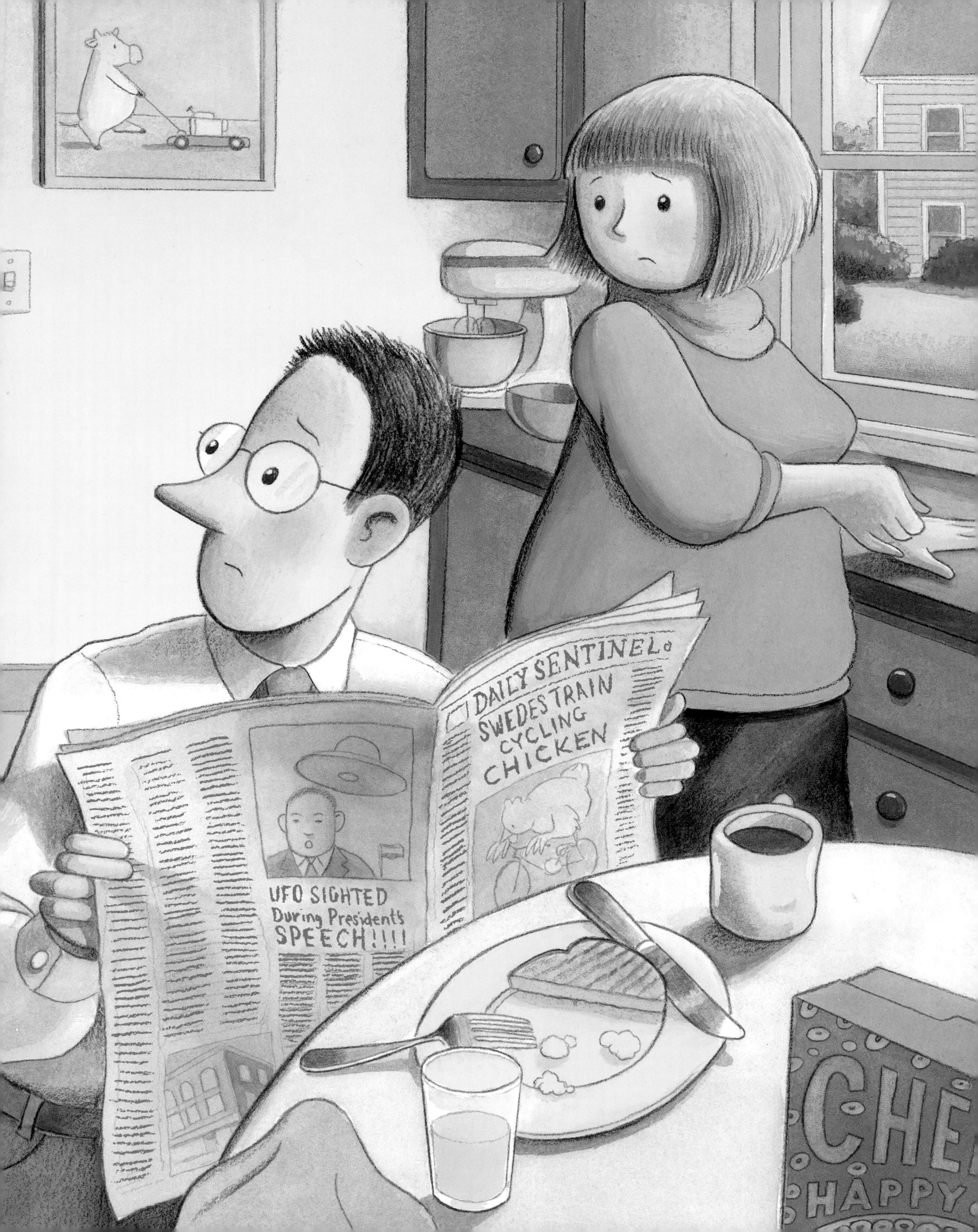
DAILY SENTINEL
SWEDES TRAIN CYCLING CHICKEN
UFO SIGHTED During President's SPEECH!!!!
CHE
HAPPY

Across Stanley's bed lay the enormous bulletin board. It had fallen on Stanley during the night. Mr. and Mrs. Lambchop hurried to lift it from the bed. But Stanley wasn't hurt.

"What's going on here?" he said cheerfully, sitting up.

"Heavens!" cried Mrs. Lambchop.

"Gosh!" said Arthur. "Stanley's flat!"

"As a pancake," said Mr. Lambchop. "Darnedest thing I've ever seen!"

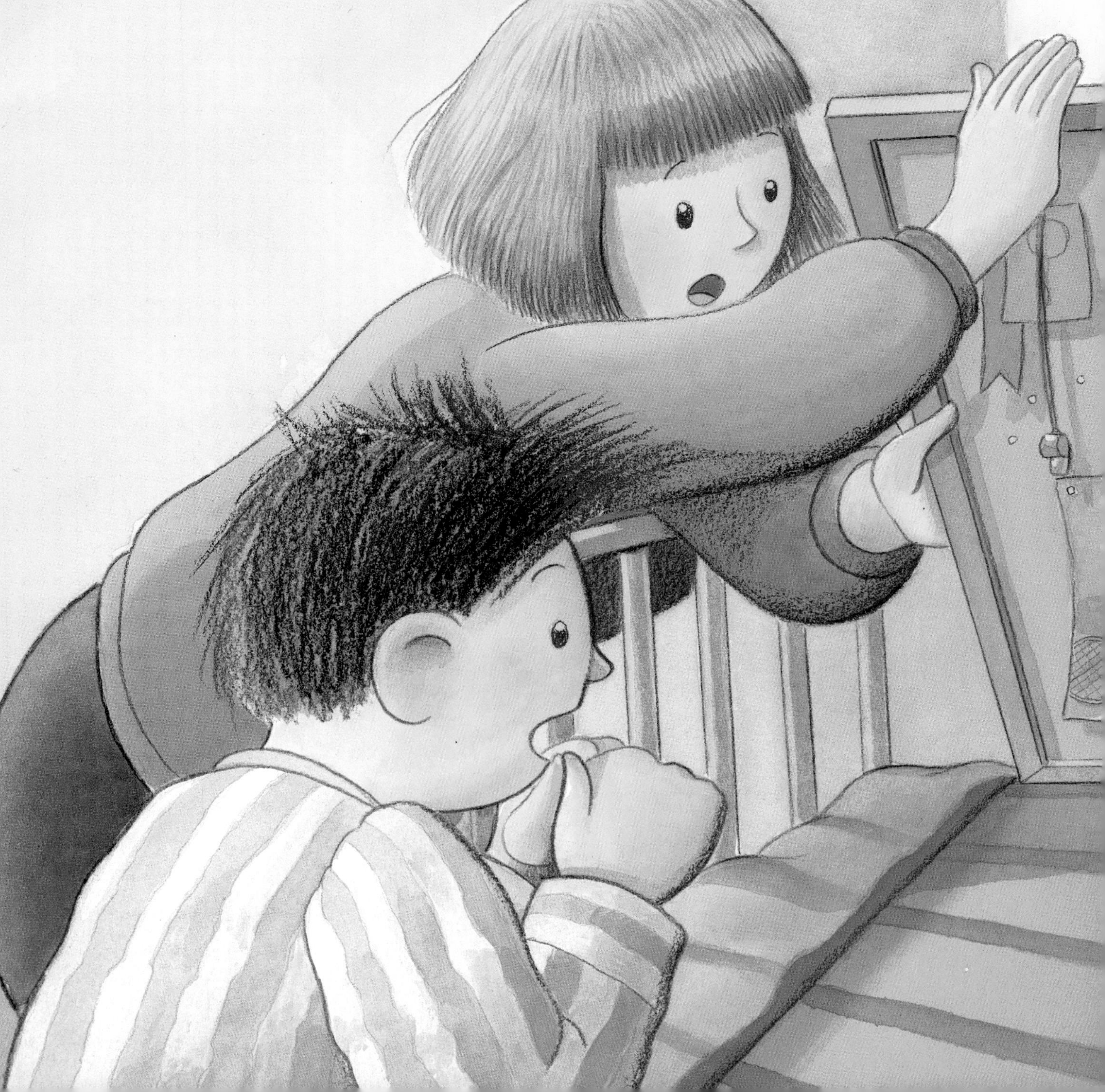

Mrs. Lambchop sighed and said, "Let's all have breakfast. Then we'll hear what Dr. Dan has to say."

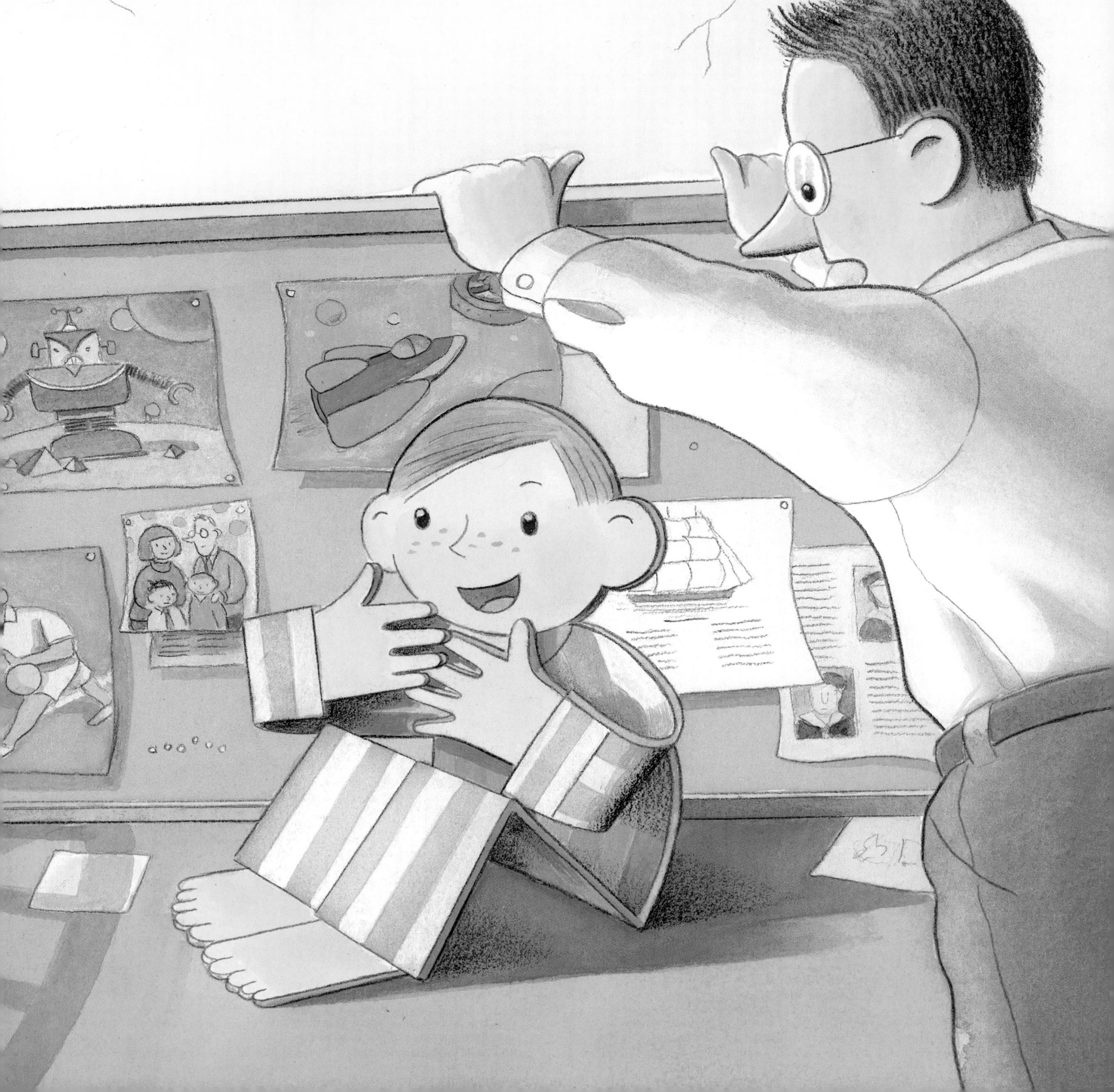

In his office, Dr. Dan examined Stanley.

"How do you feel?" he asked.

"I felt sort of tickly after I got up," Stanley said. "But I feel fine now."

"Well, that's mostly how it is with these cases," said Dr. Dan.

The nurses took Stanley's measurements.

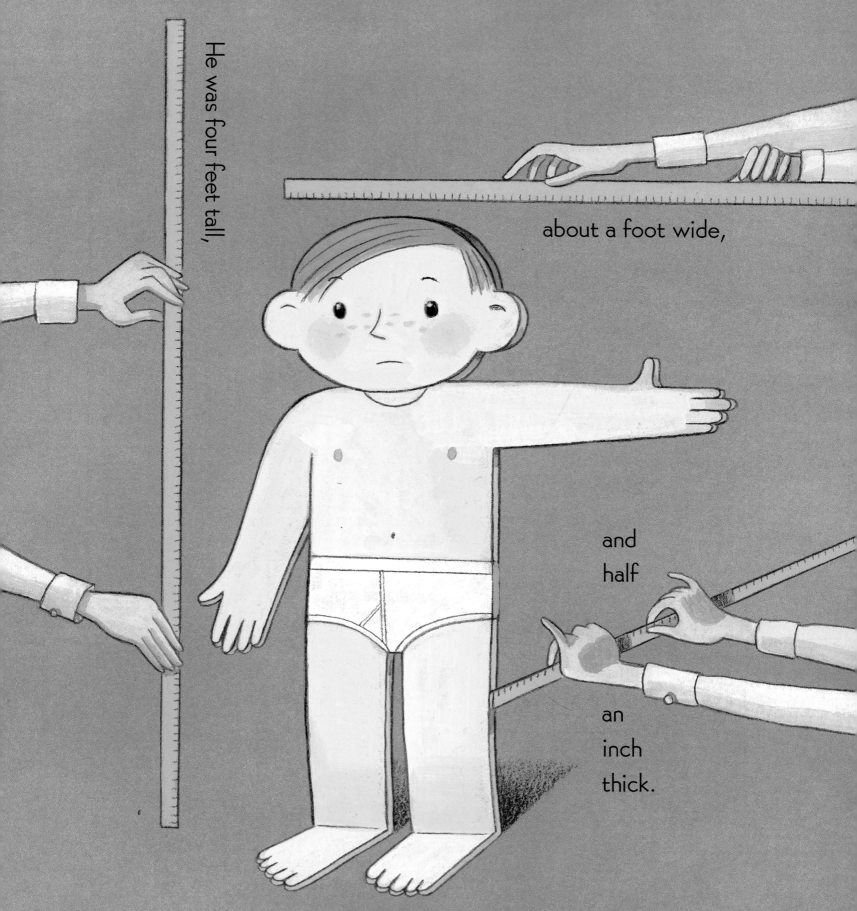

He was four feet tall,

about a foot wide,

and half an inch thick.

**Being flat could be fun.** Stanley enjoyed going in and out of rooms by sliding through the crack at the bottom of the door. Arthur tried too, but he just banged his head.

**Being flat could be exciting.** During the holidays, Stanley was invited to visit his friend Thomas in California. Mr. Lambchop brought home an enormous brown paper envelope and said, "Stanley, try this on for size."
The envelope fit Stanley perfectly, and the next morning his parents slid him into it, along with an egg-salad sandwich, and mailed him from the box on the corner.

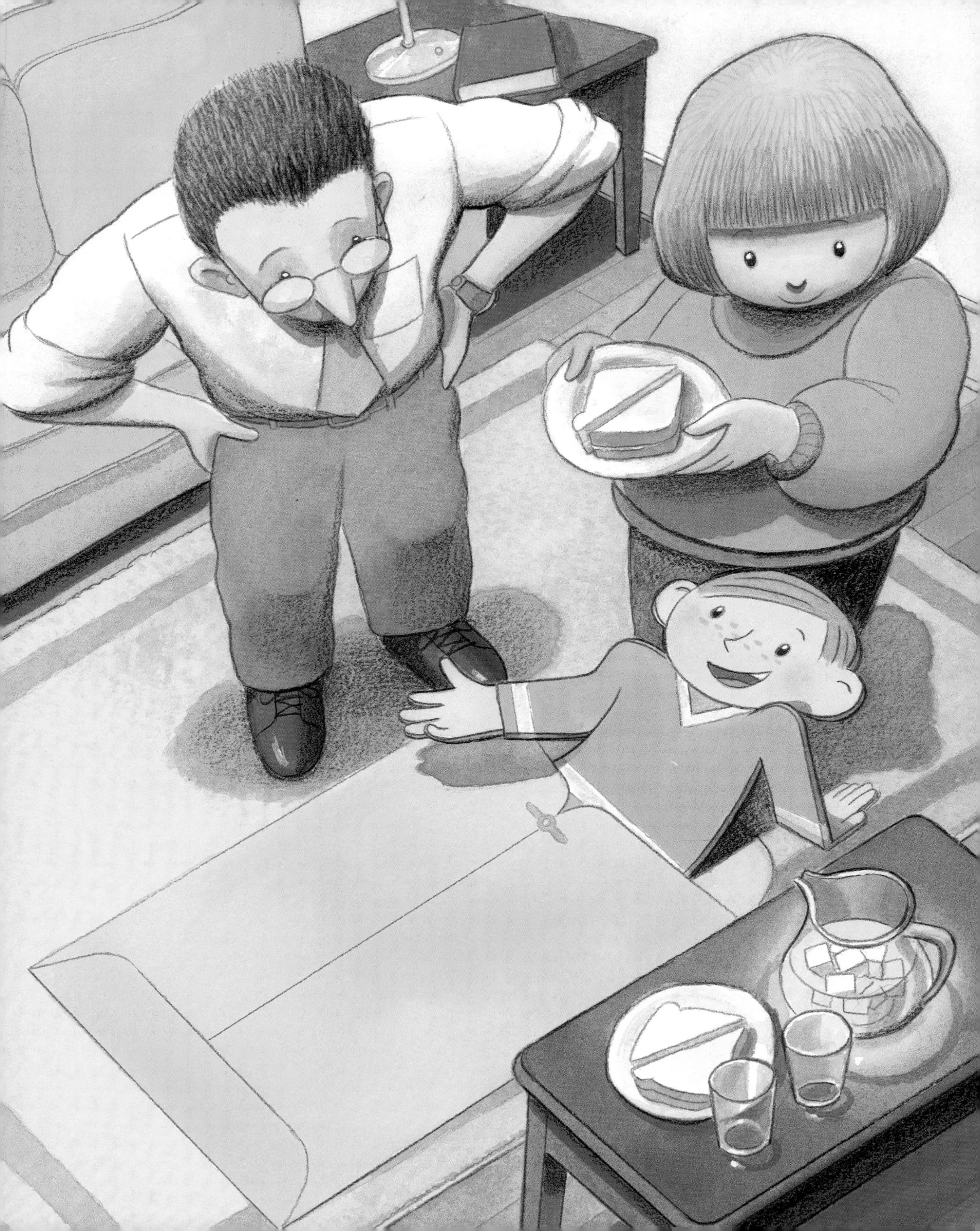

Stanley had a fine time in California.

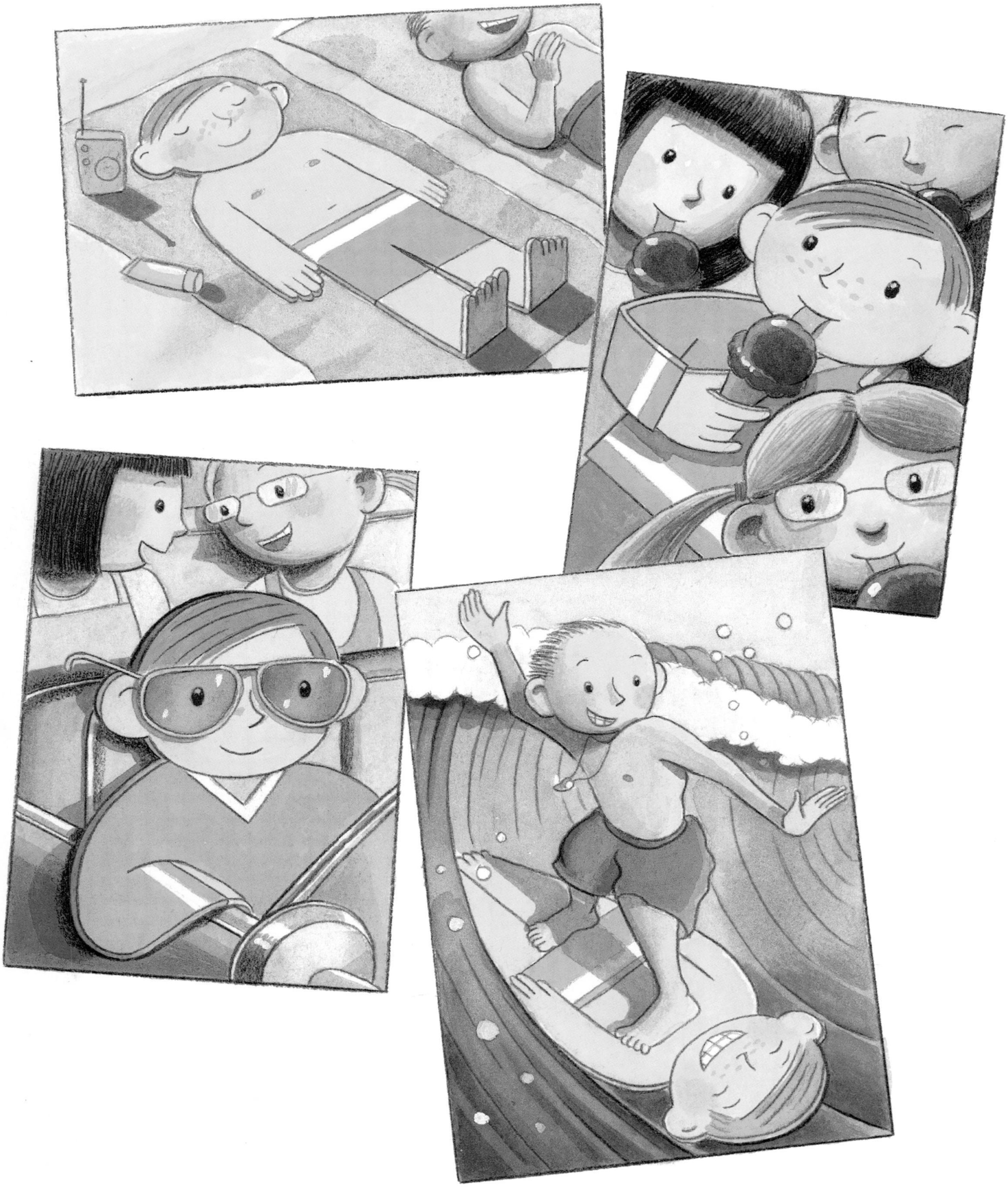

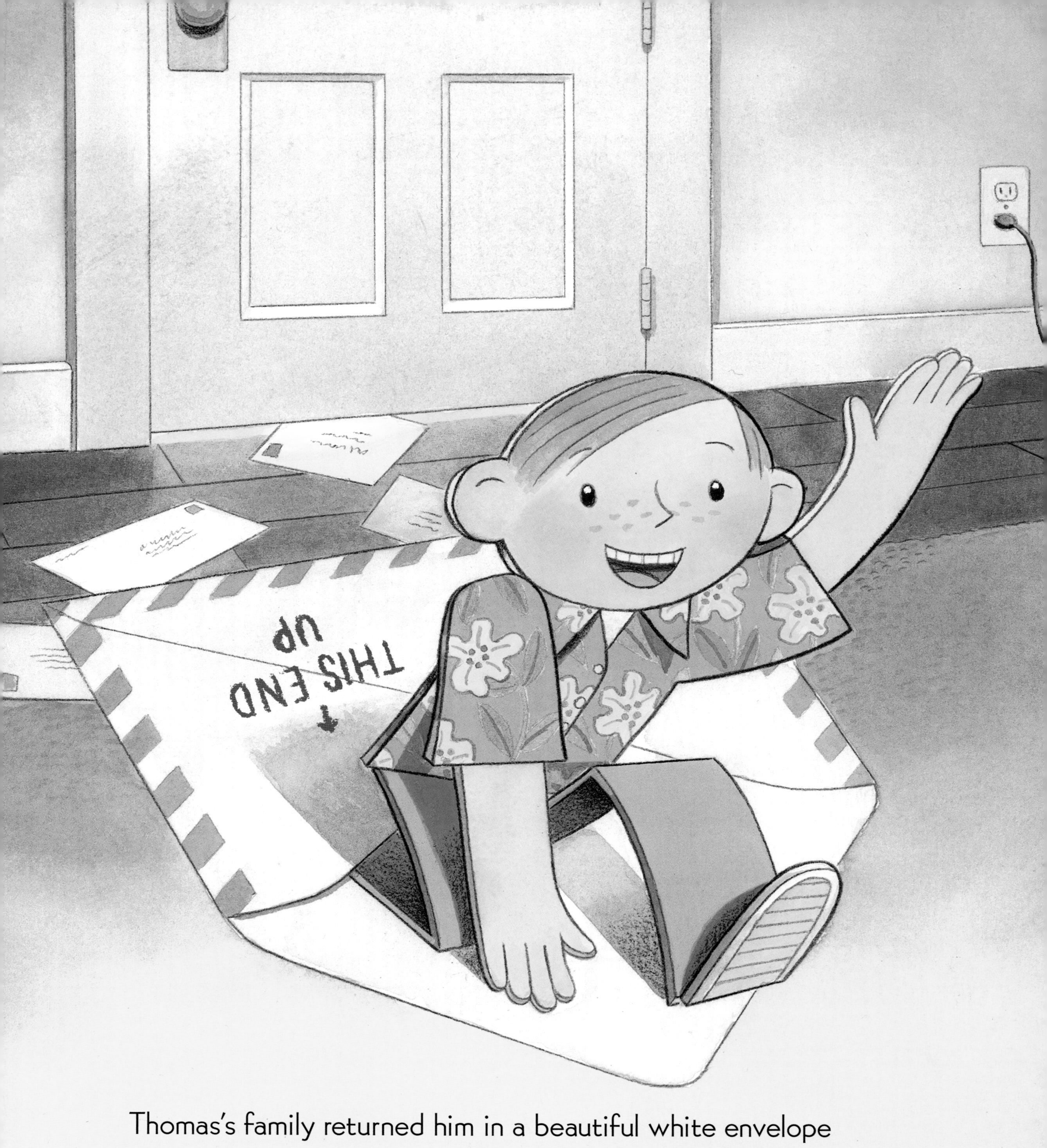
THIS END
UP

Thomas's family returned him in a beautiful white envelope they had made themselves. They marked it AIRMAIL and wrote VALUABLE and THIS END UP on both sides.

In the park one Sunday afternoon, Stanley and Arthur watched some boys flying big kites.

"Some day," Arthur said, "I would like to have a big kite."

"You can fly me, Arthur," Stanley said. "Come on!"

He gave Arthur a spool of string and attached the string to himself. Then he ran across the grass to catch the wind.

Up, up, up! went Stanley. Arthur let out all the string, and Stanley soared high above the trees. Everyone stood still to watch.

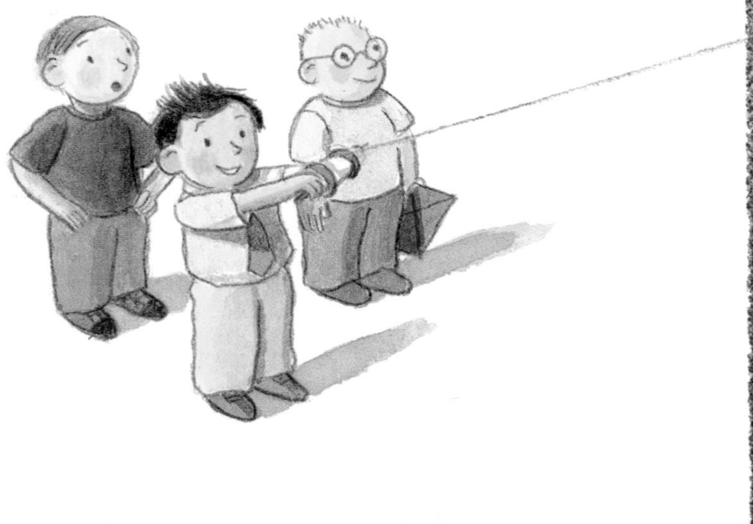

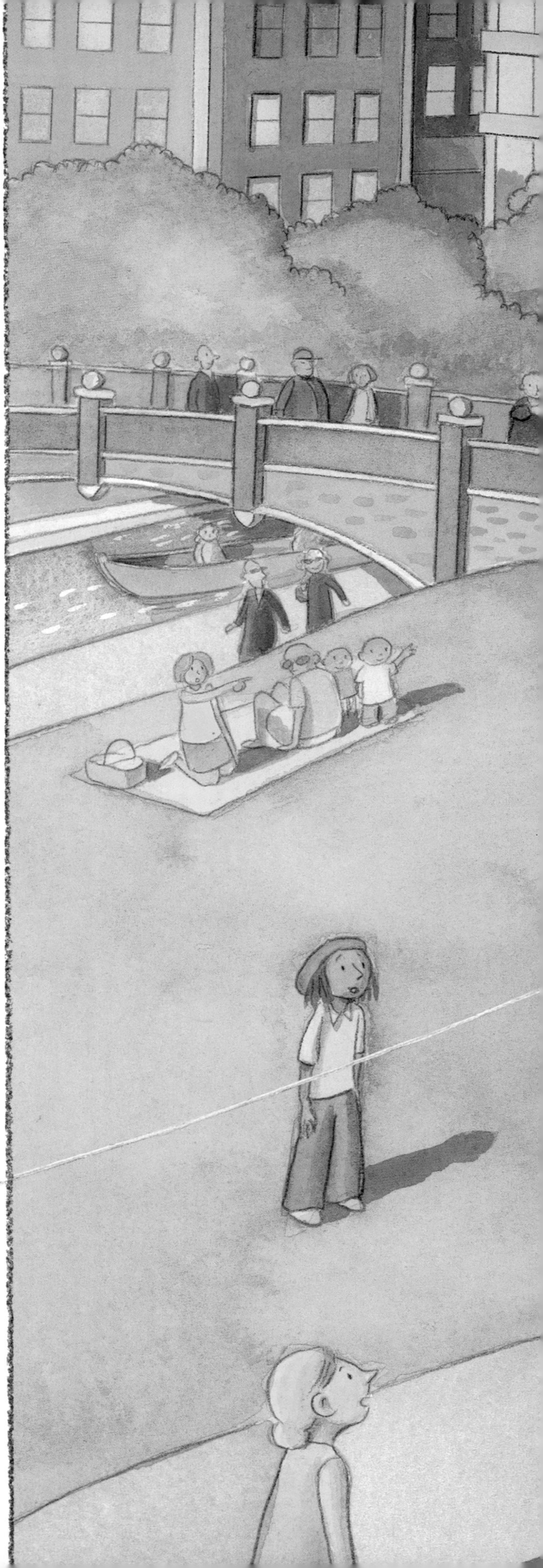

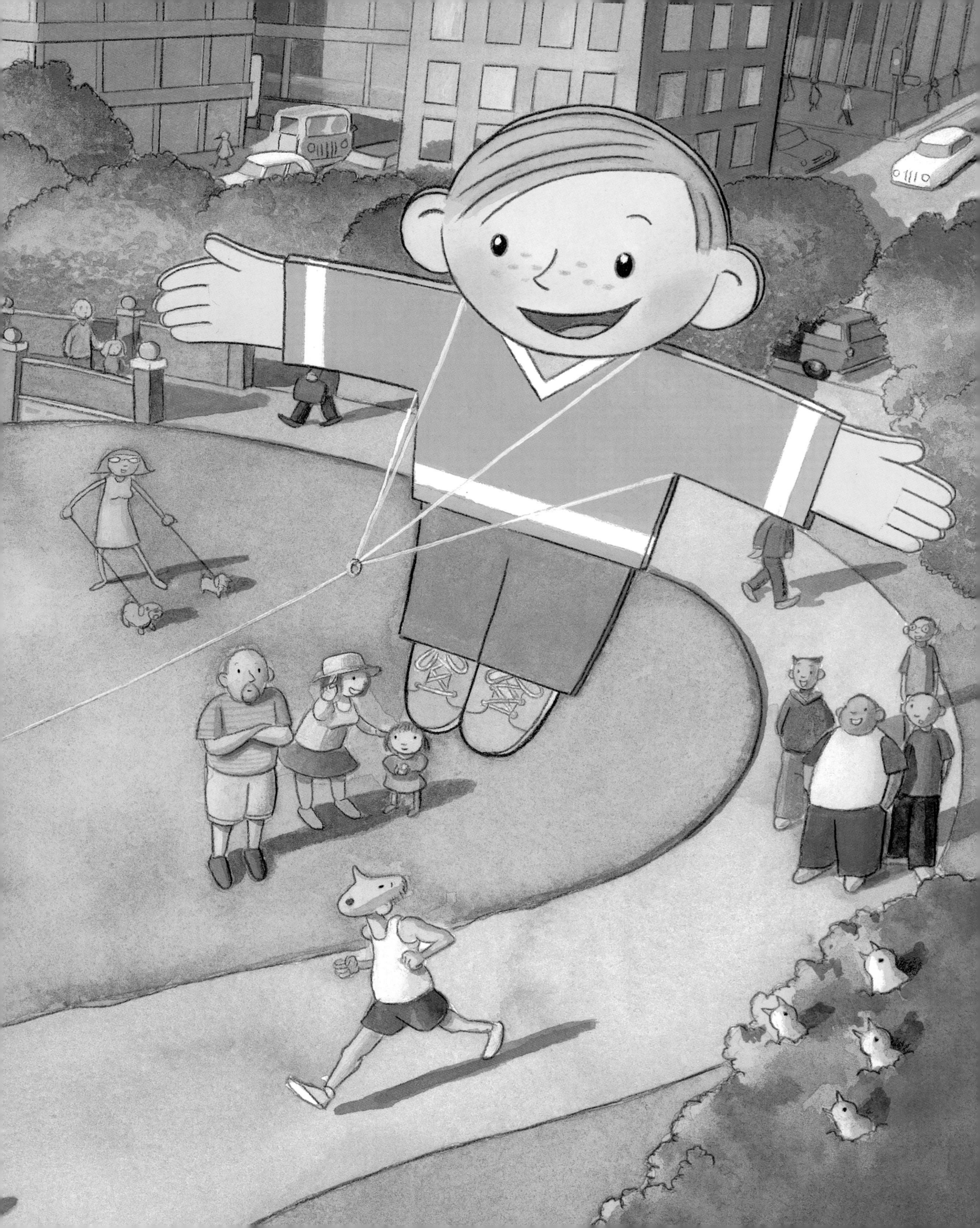

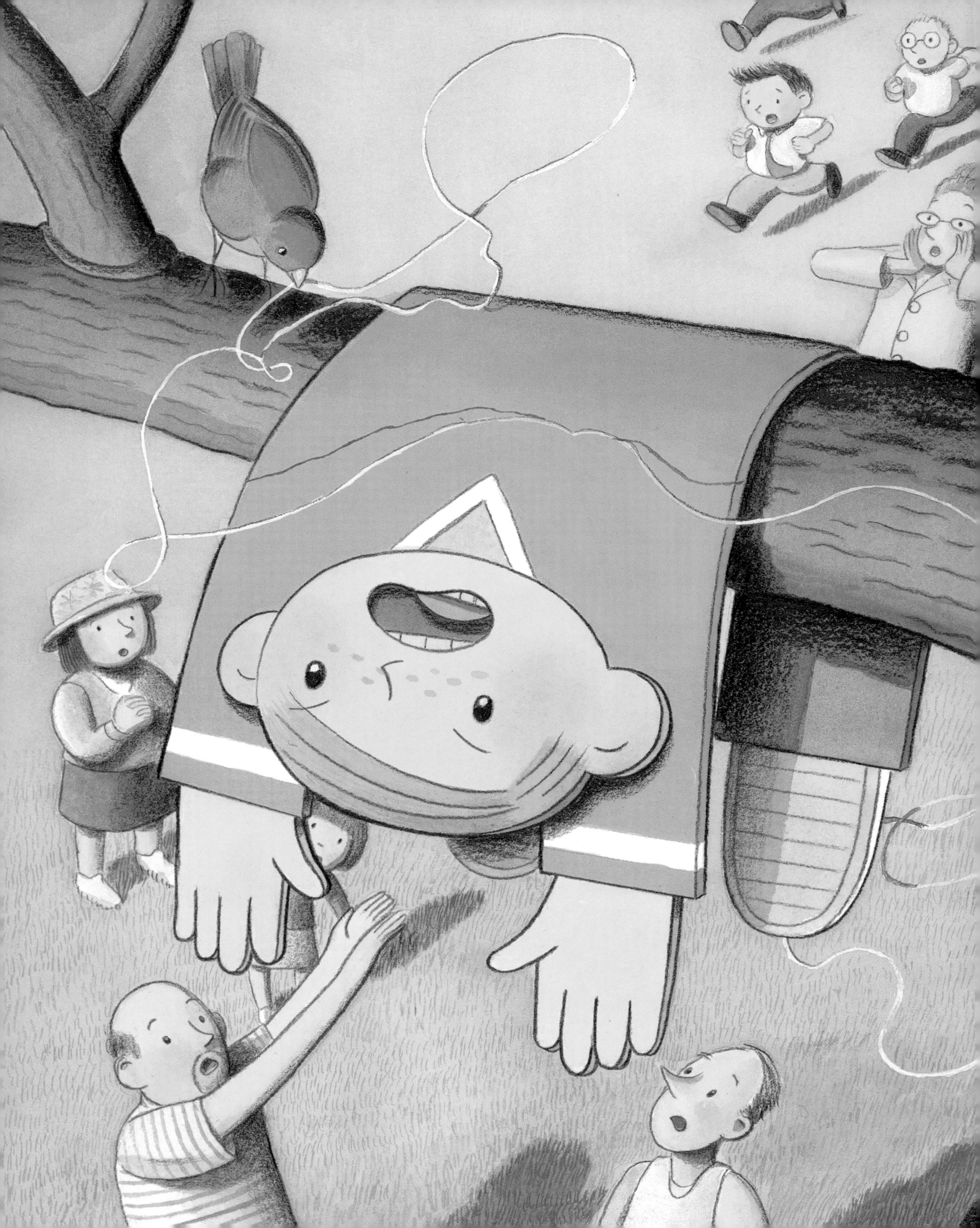

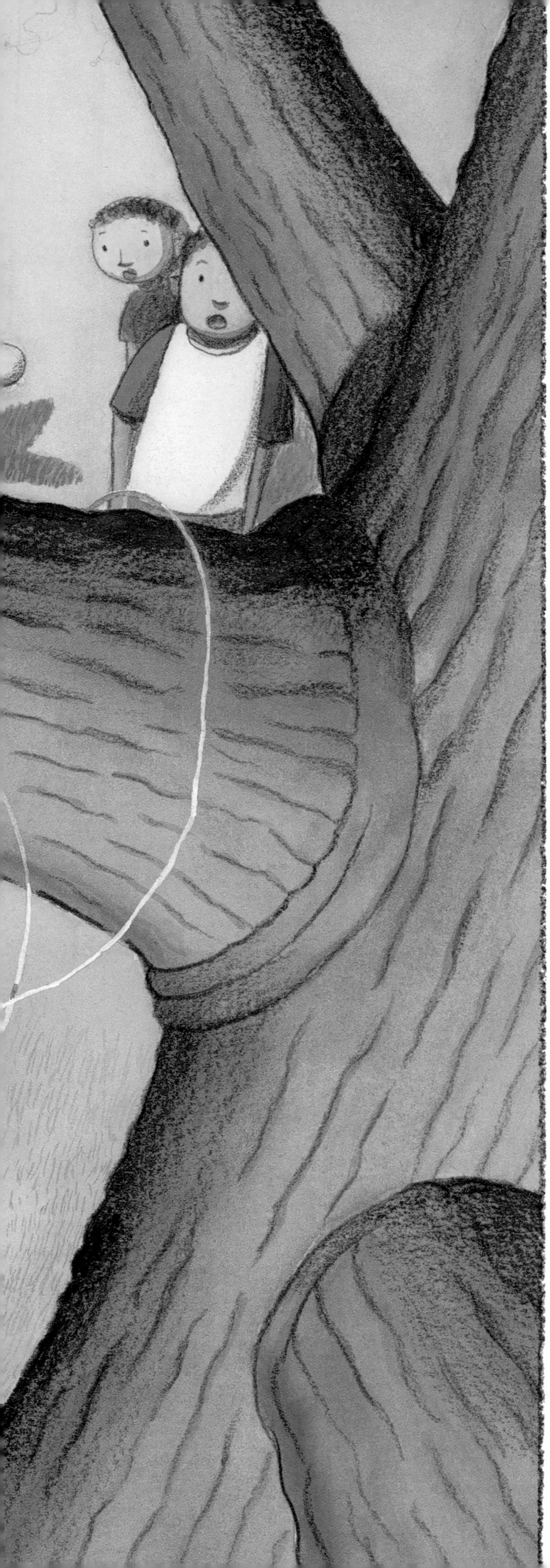

But Arthur got tired of running with the empty spool. Wedging it in the fork of a tree, he went off for a hot dog. He didn't notice when Stanley became tangled in the branches of the tree. Half an hour passed before Arthur heard Stanley's shouts and climbed up to set him free.

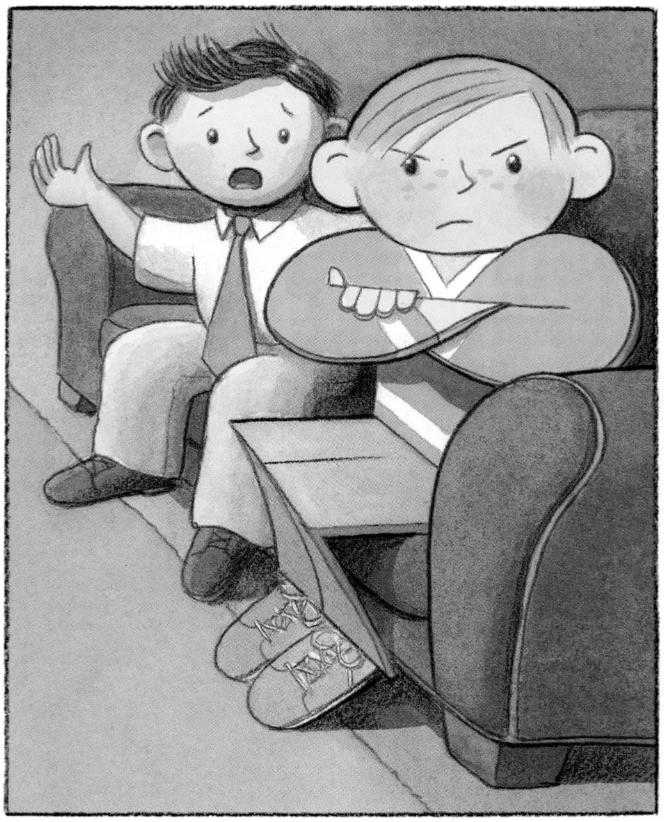

Arthur apologized over and over again that evening. But Stanley was still cross.

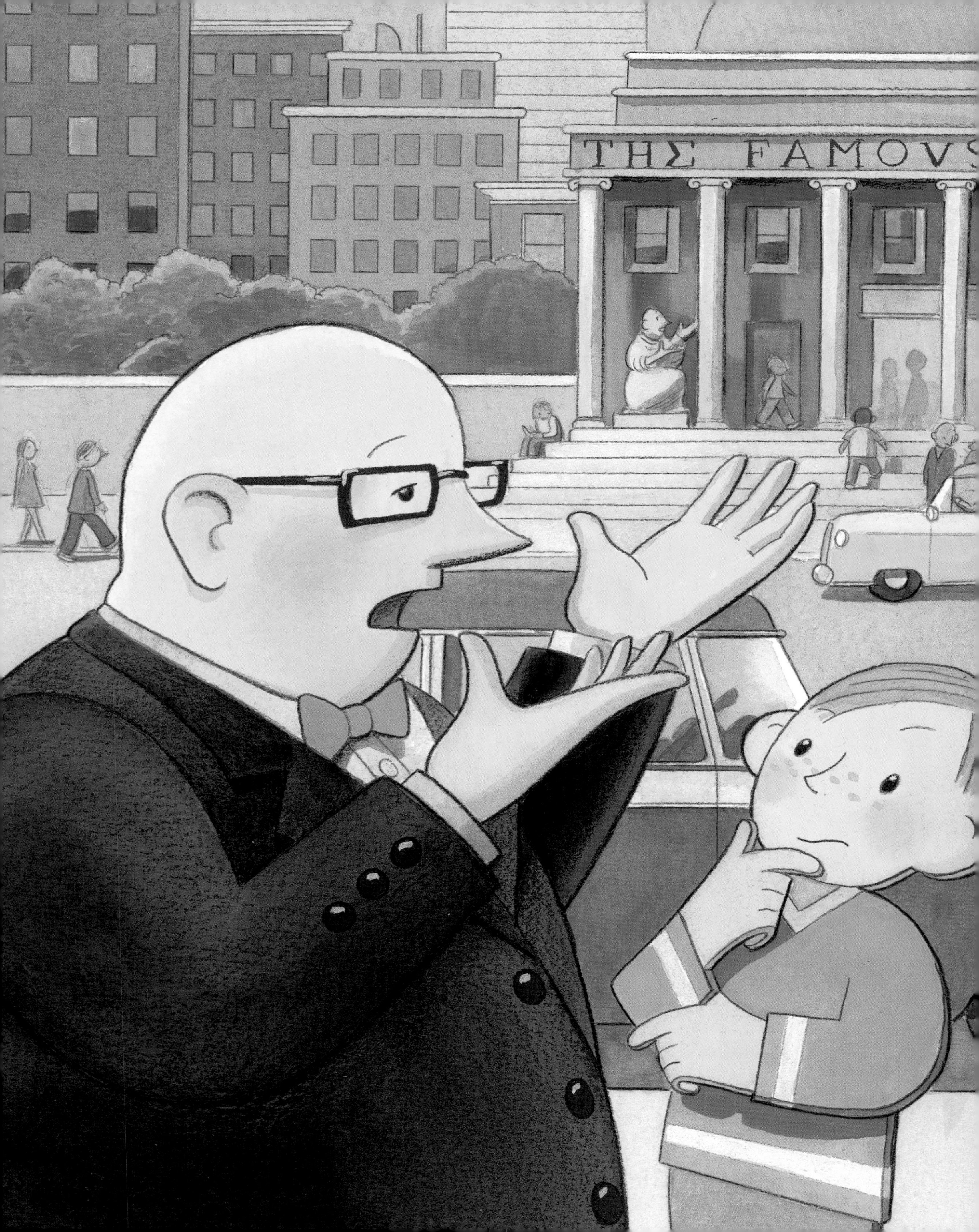
THE FAMOUS

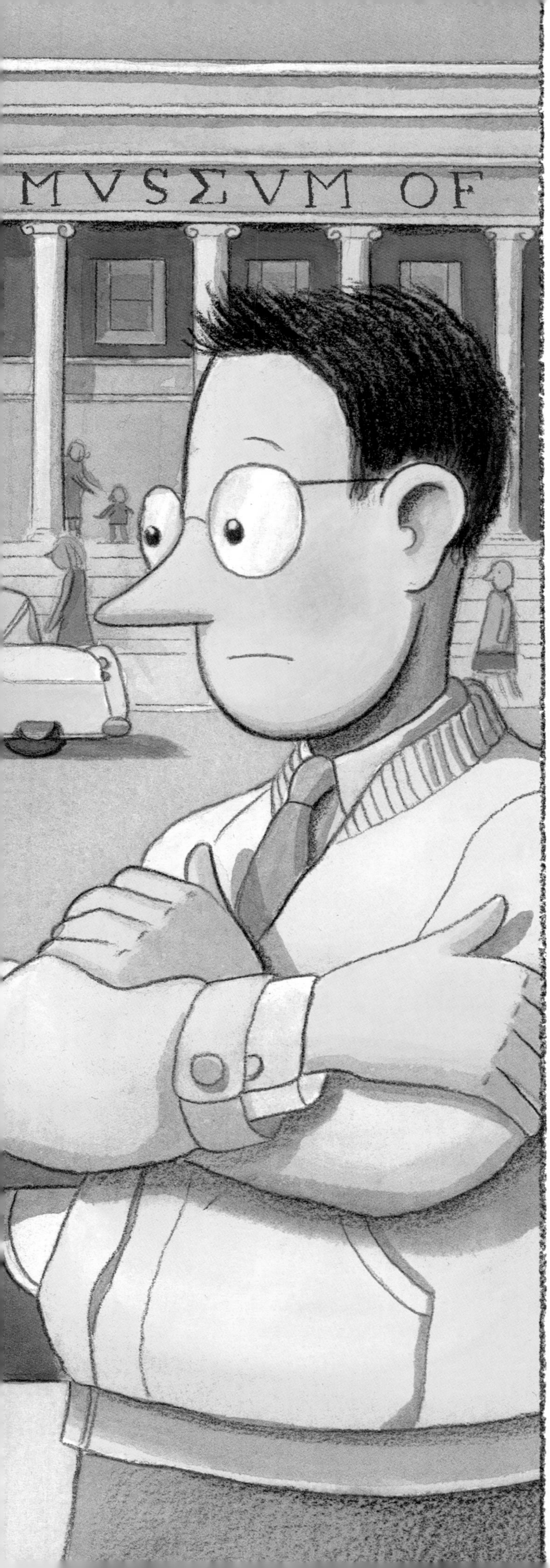
MVSΣVM OF

The next morning, Mr. Lambchop and Stanley met their neighbor Mr. O. J. Dart, director of The Famous Museum of Art. Mr. Dart looked worried.

"Another valuable painting was stolen from The Famous Museum last night!" he told Stanley and his father. "The police suspect a gang of sneak thieves. They work at night by sneakery, which makes them very difficult to catch!"

Stanley had an idea. He explained it to Mr. Dart.

"Excellent!" said Mr. Dart. "We'll try out your plan tonight."

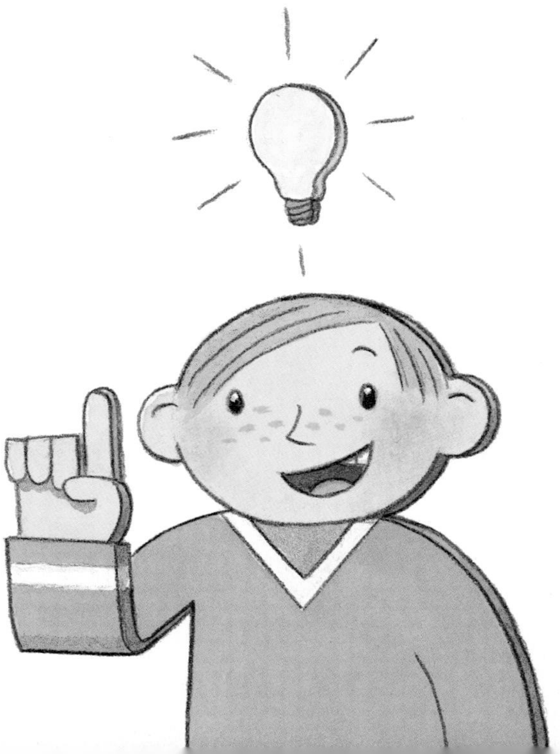

That evening in the main hall of the museum, Mr. Dart showed Stanley the most expensive painting in the world! Next to it was an empty picture frame.
"And now, Stanley," said Mr. Dart, "it's time for your disguise."

Stanley showed Mr. Dart the disguise he had brought.
"This is a really good one! My cowboy hat. And a red bandana!"
"I'm sorry," Mr. Dart said, "but we don't have cowboy pictures here. You must wear the disguise I have chosen."
Stanley could hardly speak when he saw Mr. Dart's disguise.
"I'll look like a girl!" he protested.
But Stanley was a good sport, so he put it on.

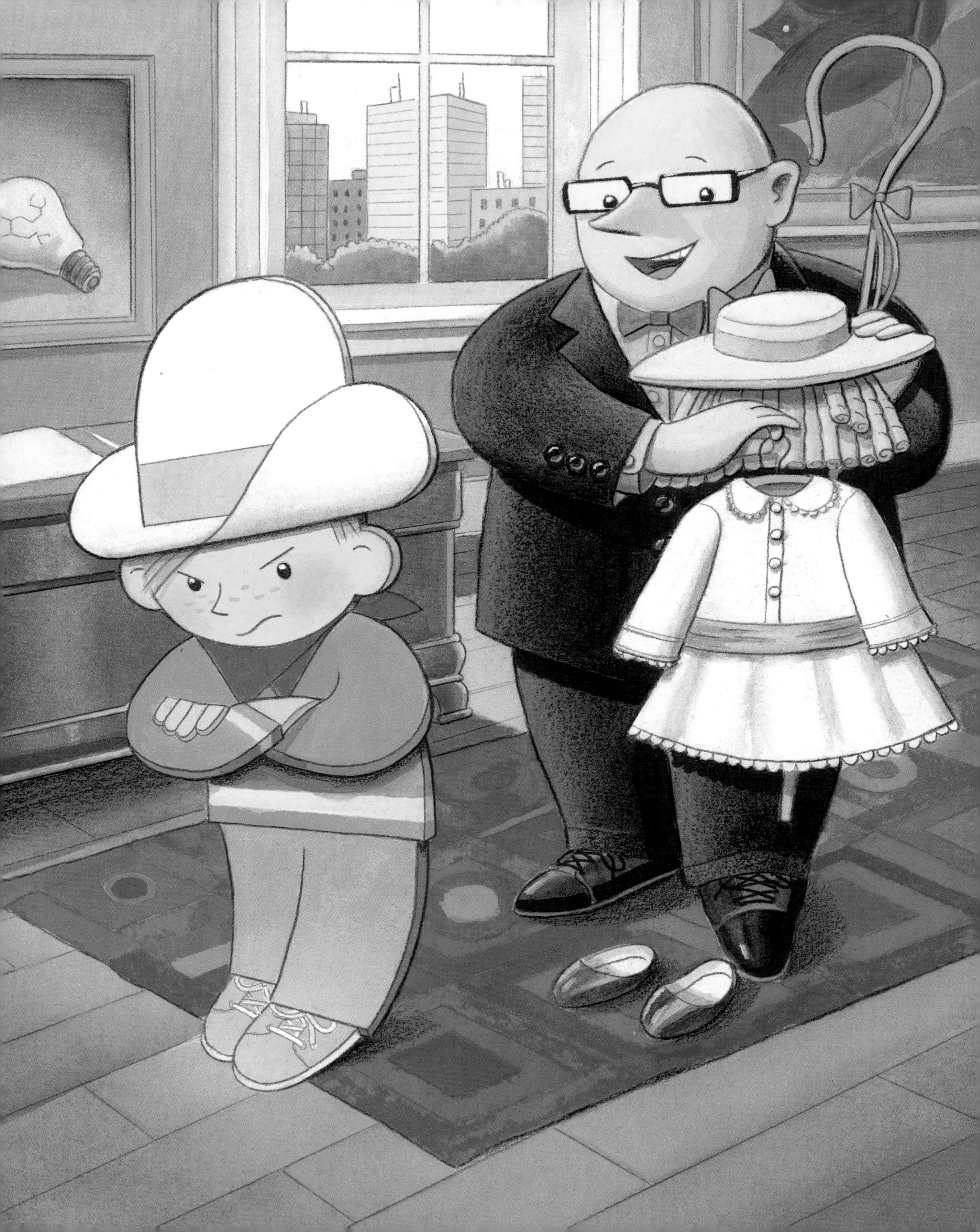

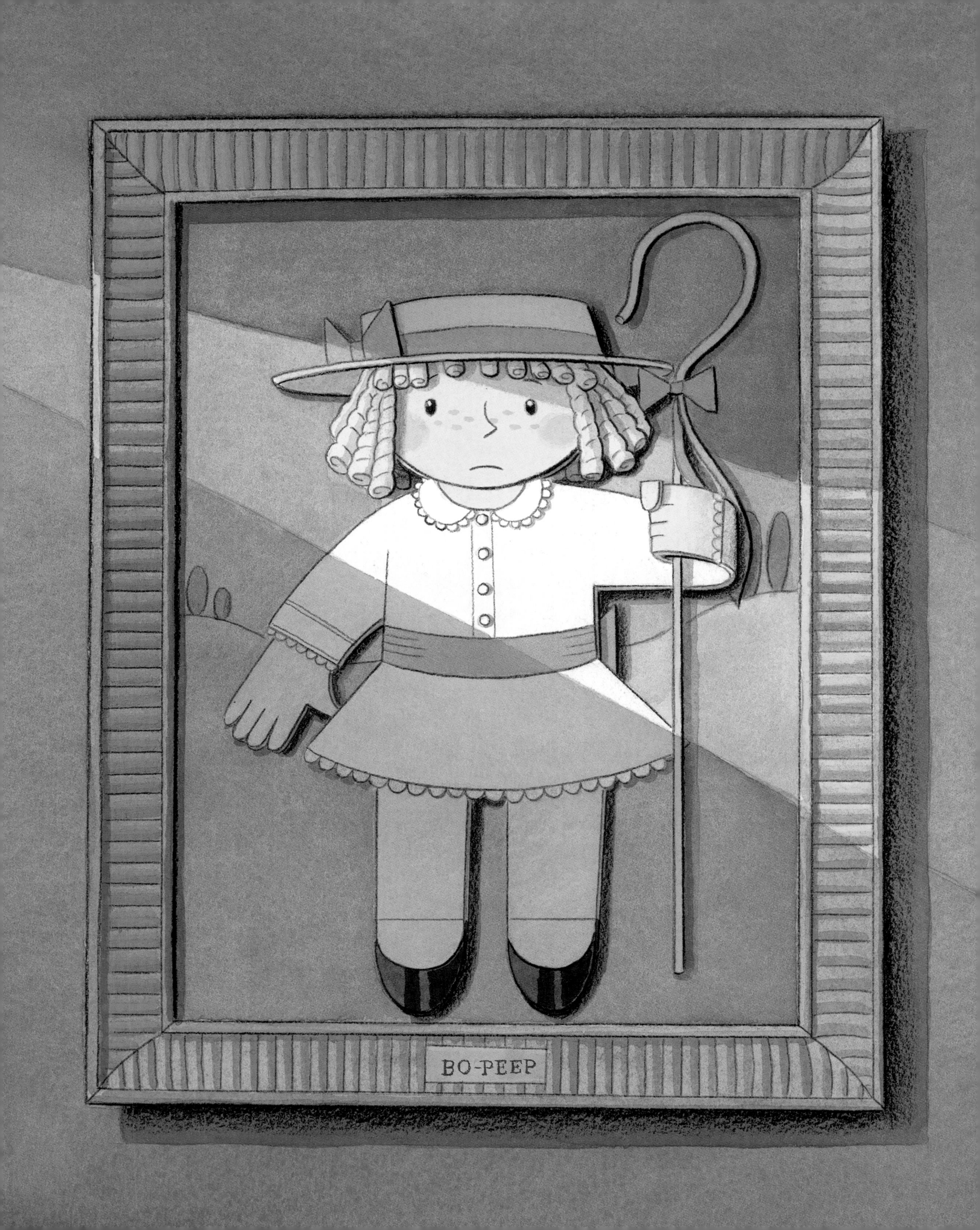
BO-PEEP

In the main hall, Stanley climbed into the empty picture frame and stood very still.

"Very nice," said Mr. Dart, and went off to arrange the rest of their plan.

Now Stanley was alone. The hall was very dark, but enough moonlight came through the windows for him to see the world's most expensive painting. Maybe the sneak thieves won't come, he thought.

Then . . .

cccccccCCRREEEEAAAAKKK

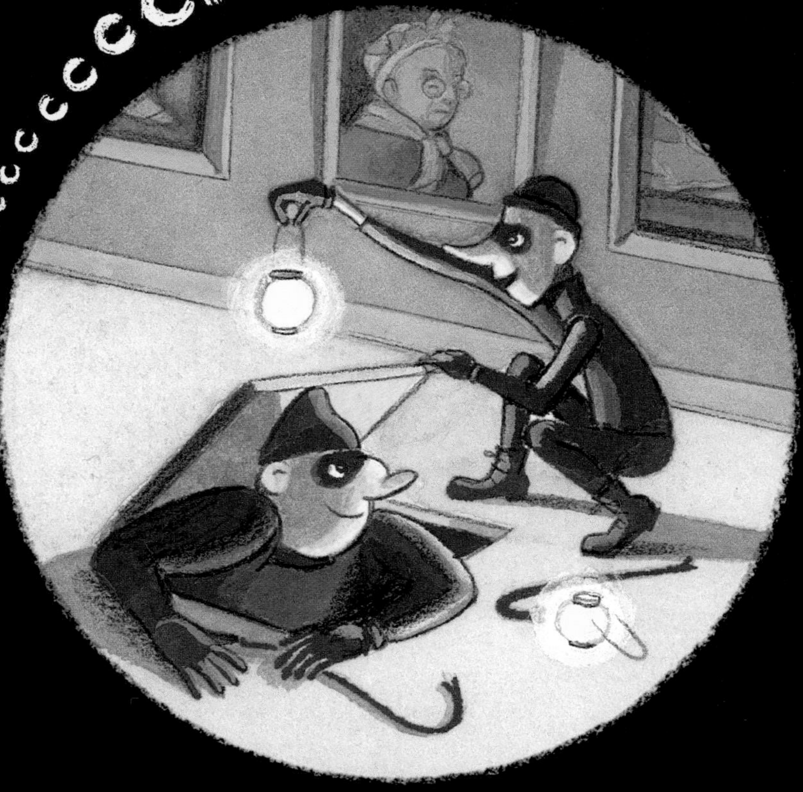

A glow of yellow light shone suddenly in the center of the hall.

A trapdoor had opened in the floor!

The sneak thieves, carrying lanterns, came up into the hall.

The thieves took the world's most expensive painting off the wall. "This is it, Max," said the first thief, whose name was Luther. "In all of this great city, there is no one to suspect us."

Then Luther saw Stanley in his frame. "I thought sheep girls were supposed to smile, Max," he said. "This one looks scared."

Stanley managed a tiny smile. "She is smiling, sort of," Max said. "And what a pretty little thing she is, too."

That made Stanley furious. In his loudest voice he shouted:

"POLICE! MR. DART! THE SNEAK THIEVES ARE HERE!"

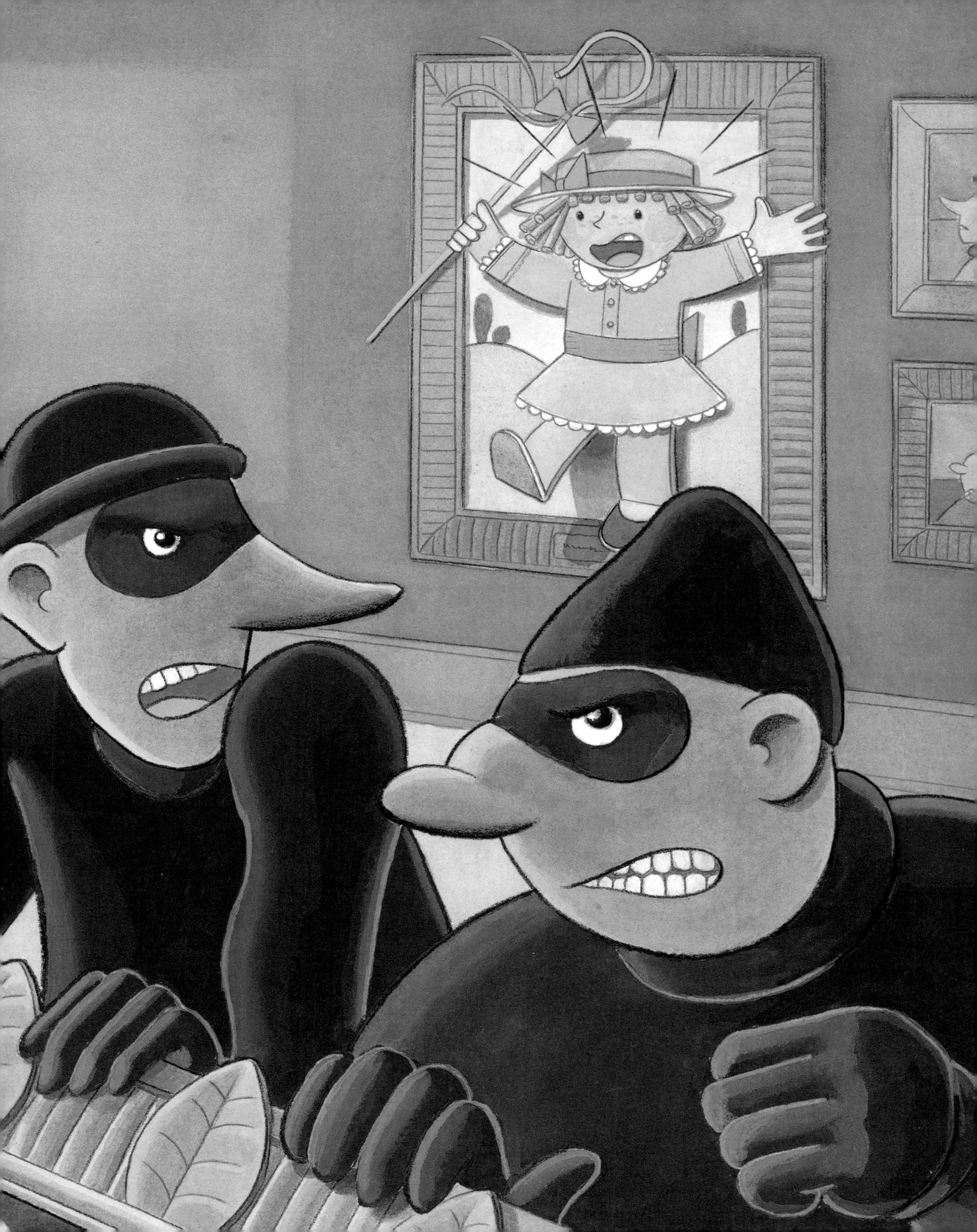

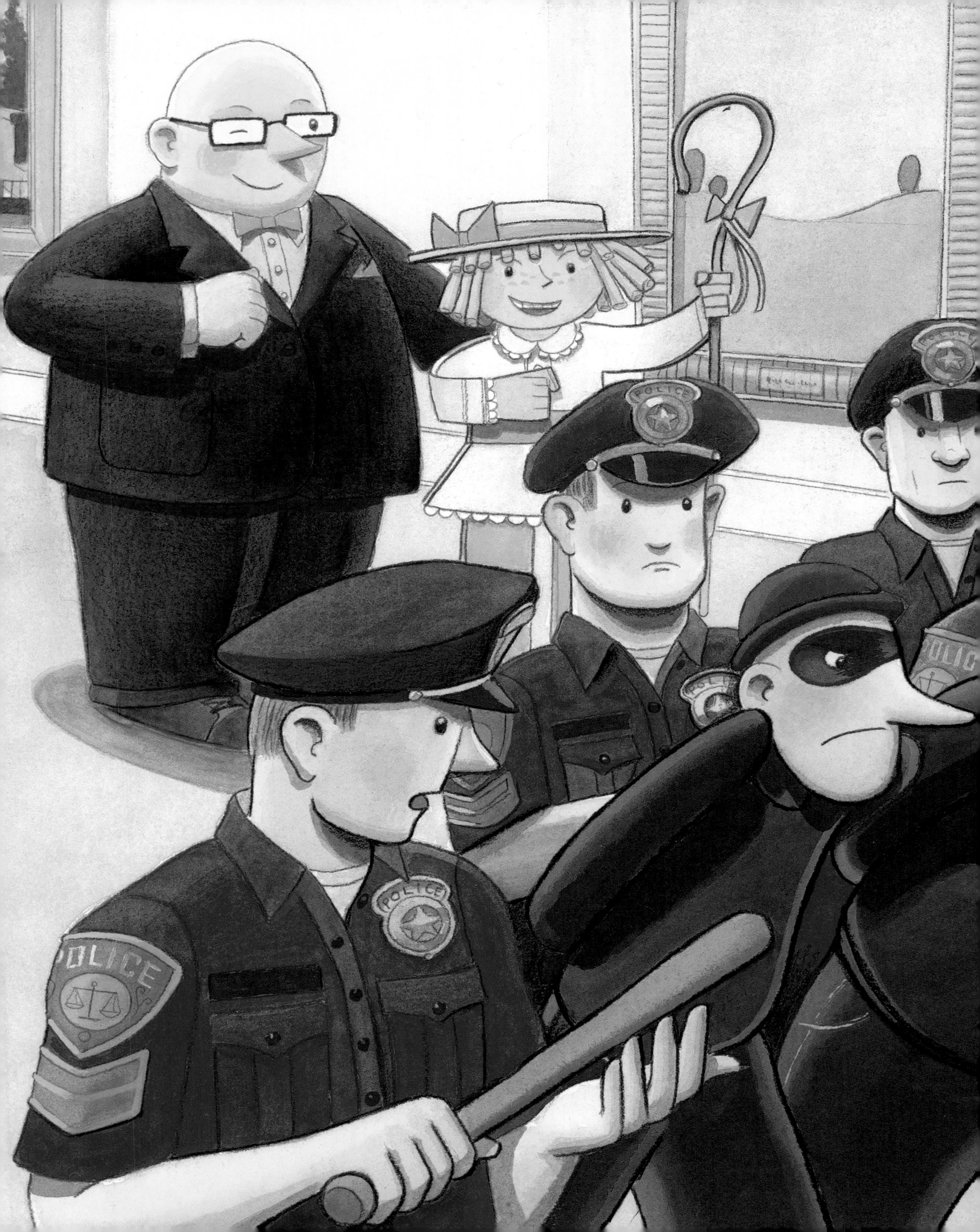
POLICE
POLICE
POLICE
POLICE
POLICE

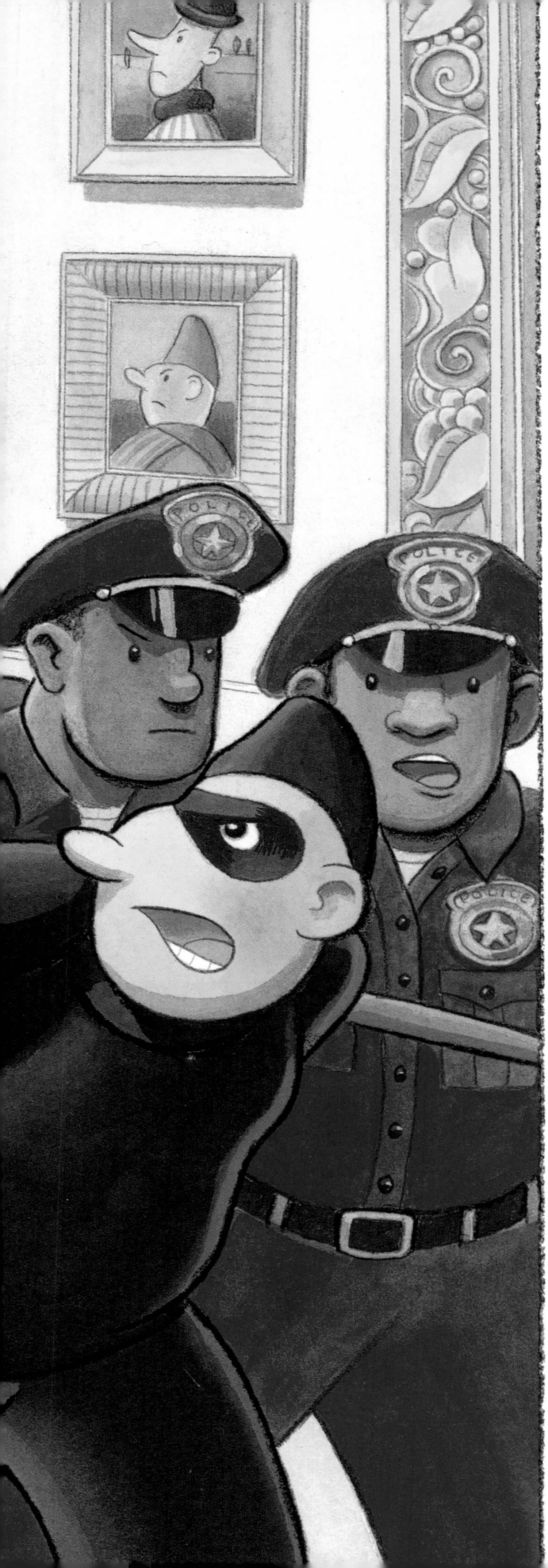
POLICE
POLICE
POLICE

"Max . . ." Luther whispered. "I think I heard the sheep girl yell."

"Oh, boy! Yelling pictures! We both need a rest," Max whispered back.

"You'll get a rest, all right!" shouted Mr. Dart, rushing in with lots of policemen. "You'll get ar-rested, that's what!"

The sneak thieves were quickly handcuffed and led away to jail.

The next morning, Stanley Lambchop got a medal from the Chief of Police. The day after that his picture was in all the newspapers.

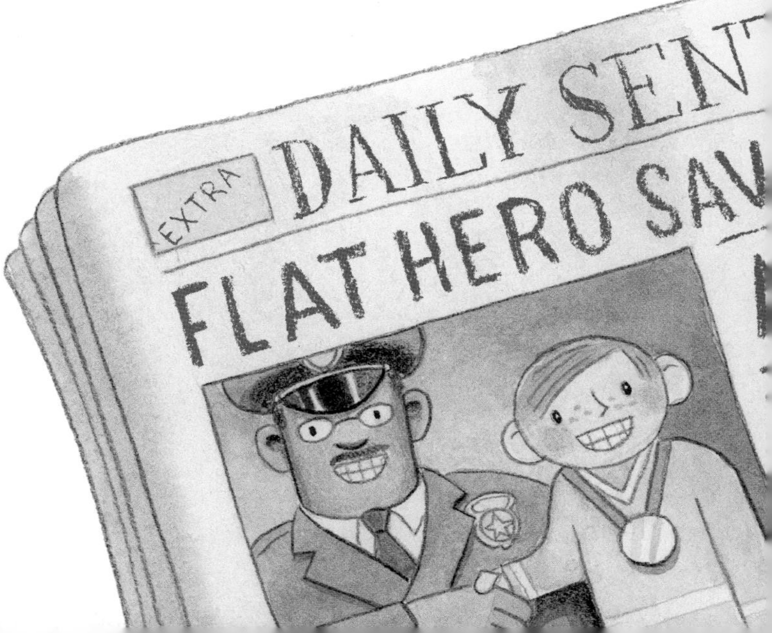
EXTRA
DAILY SEN
FLAT HERO SAV

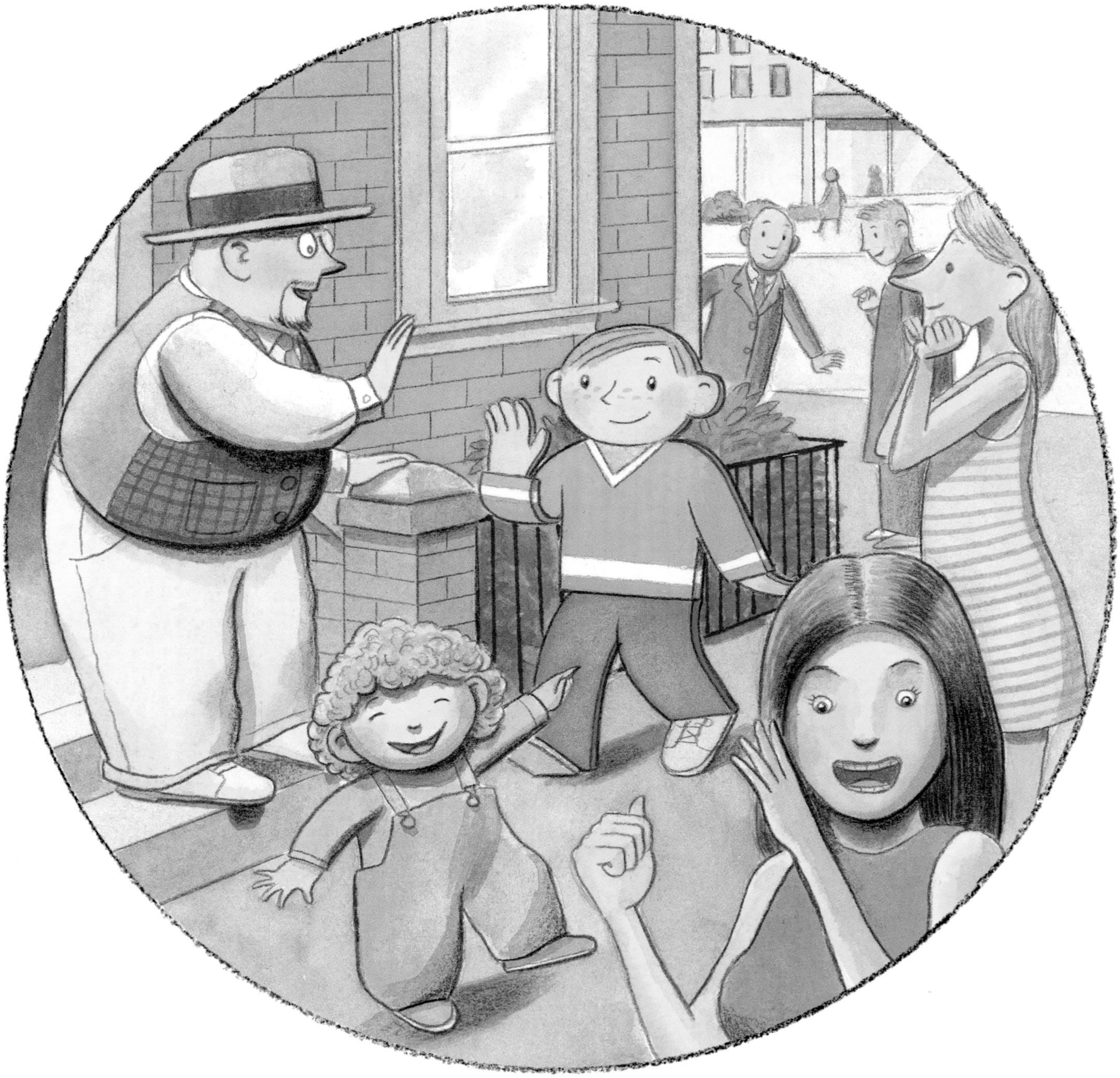

For a while Stanley was famous. People would point him out and whisper, "Over there, Agnes! Stanley Lambchop, the one who caught the museum robbers . . ."
And things like that.

But then people began to make fun of him. "Hi, Super-skinny!" they would call.

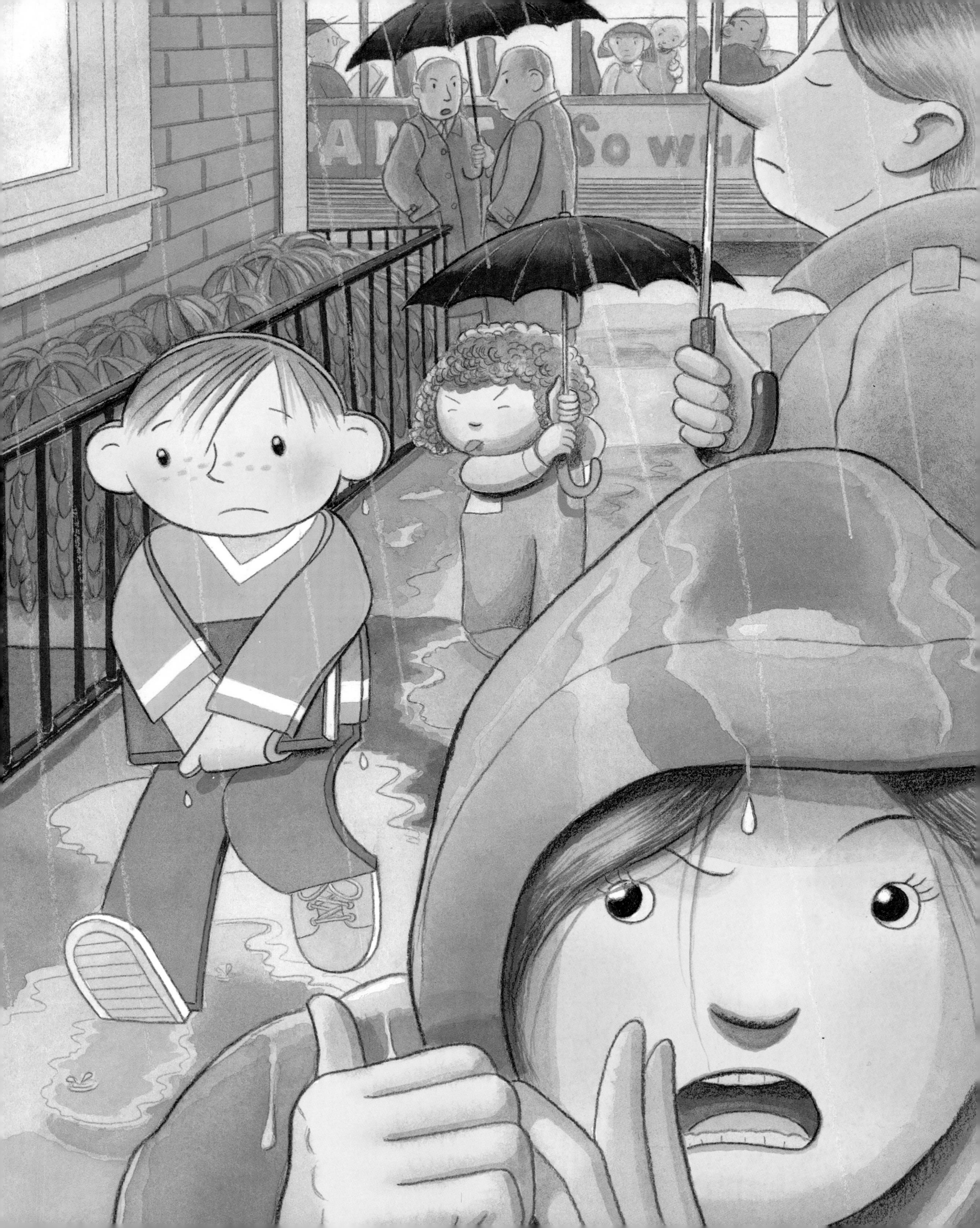

Late one night, Arthur woke to the sound of Stanley crying.
"What's wrong?" he said.
Stanley sighed. "I want to be a regular shape again, like other people. It's not fair."
"You're brave," Arthur said. "You really are."

And then Arthur had an idea. He turned on the light, and ran to the big toy box in the corner. He tossed aside toy soldiers, airplanes, and boat models.
"Got it!" he said, holding up an old bicycle pump.

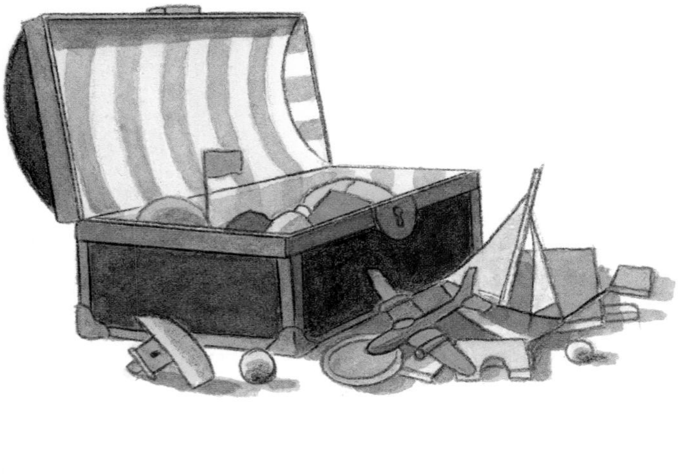

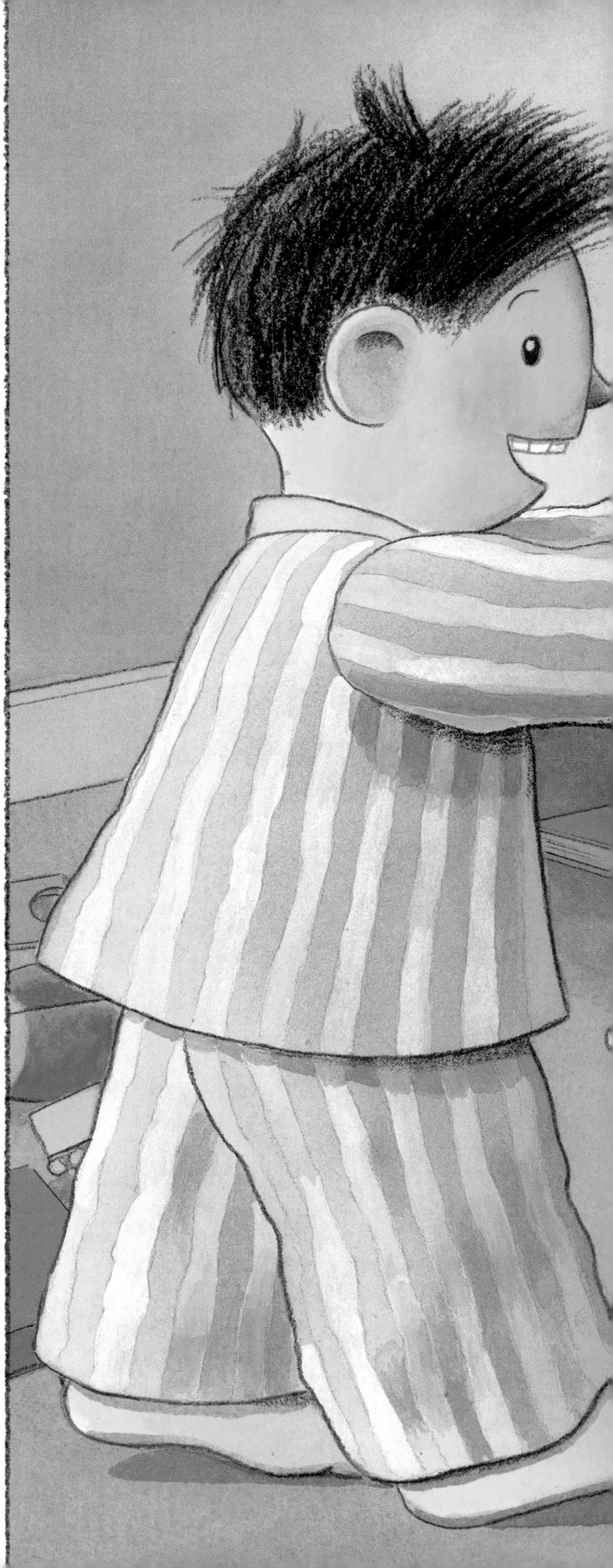

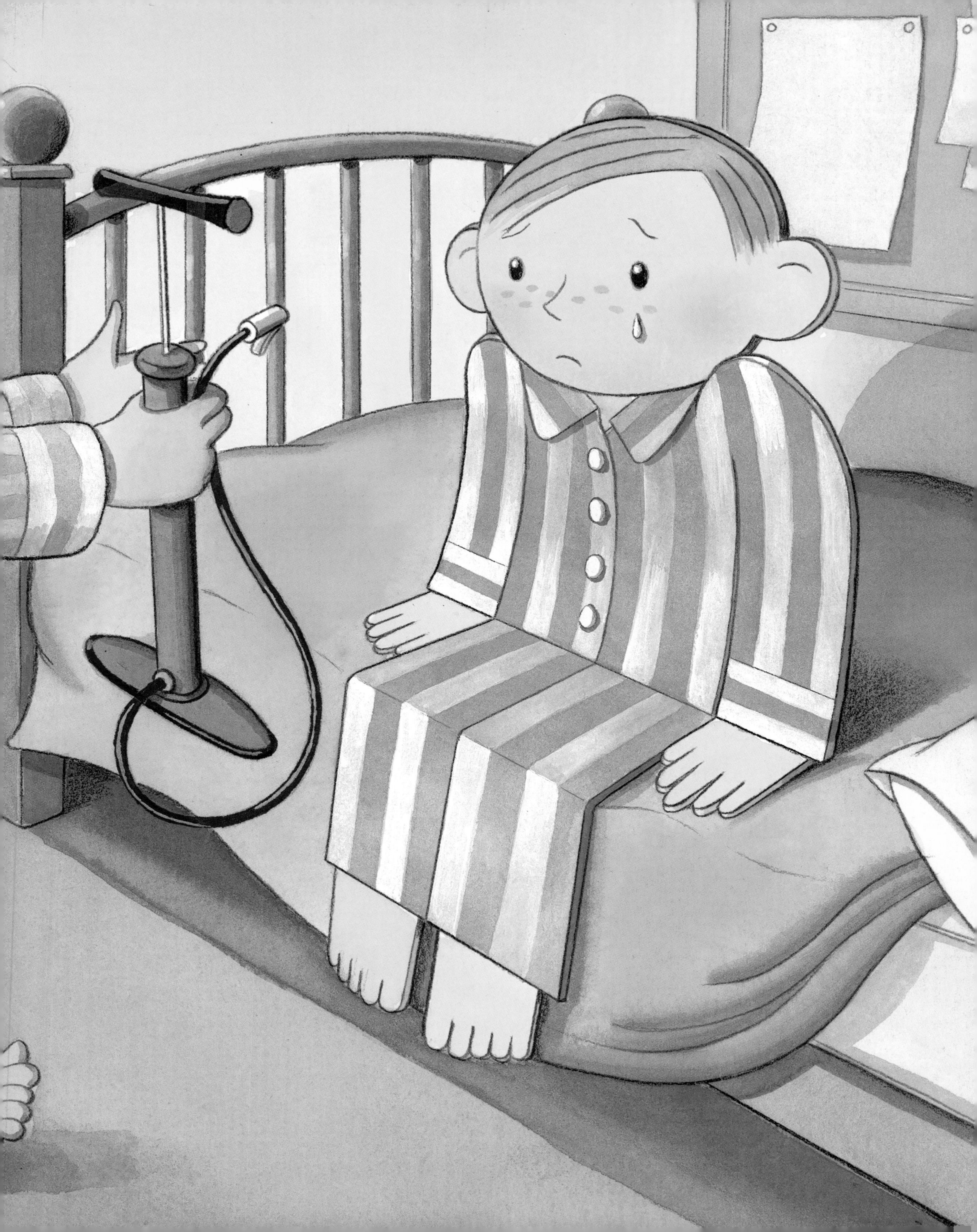

"OK," Stanley said after a moment. "But take it easy." He stood with the end of the hose in his mouth, clamping his lips tightly so no air could escape. Arthur began to pump. "If it hurts or anything, wiggle your hand," he said. Stanley's top half began to swell.

Stanley got

BIGGER

and

BIGGER.

His pajama buttons

burst off —

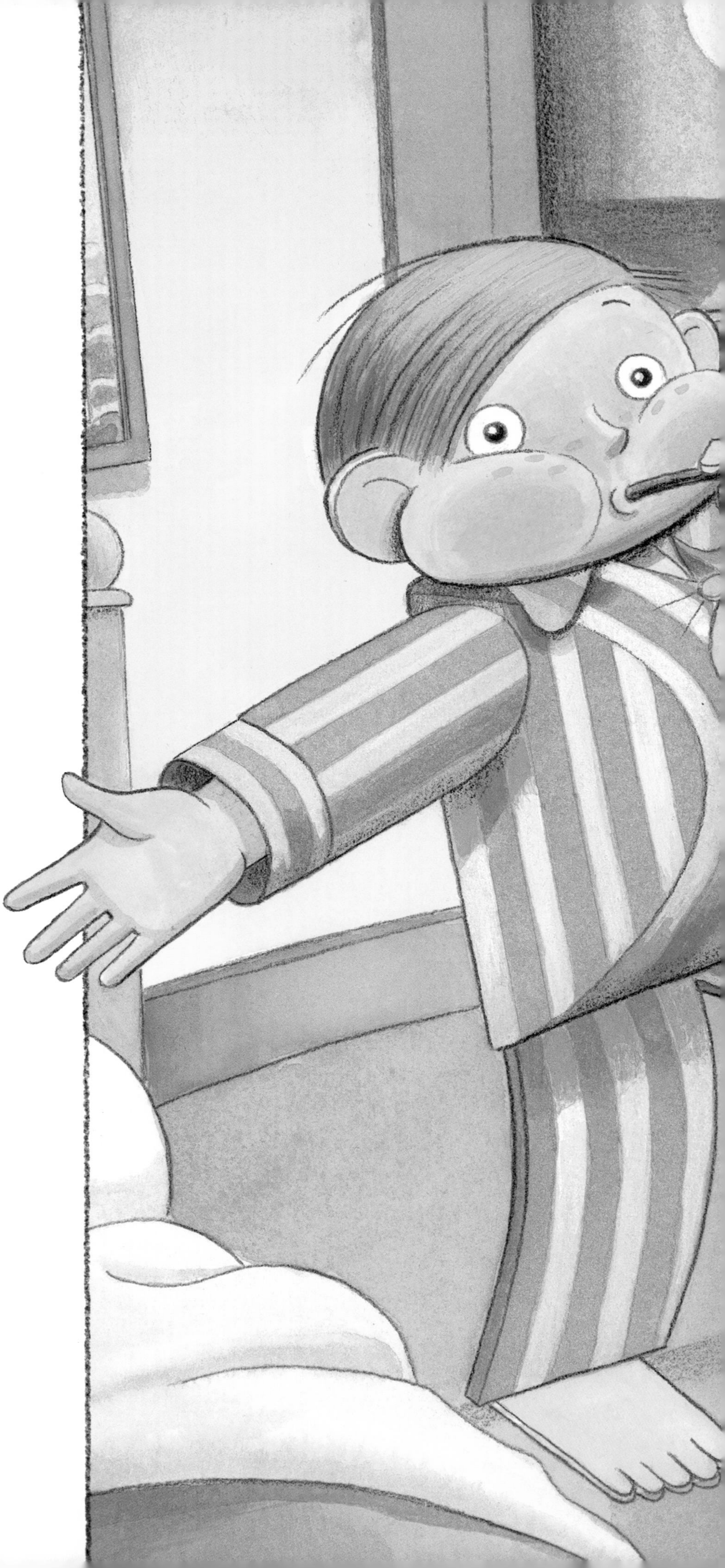

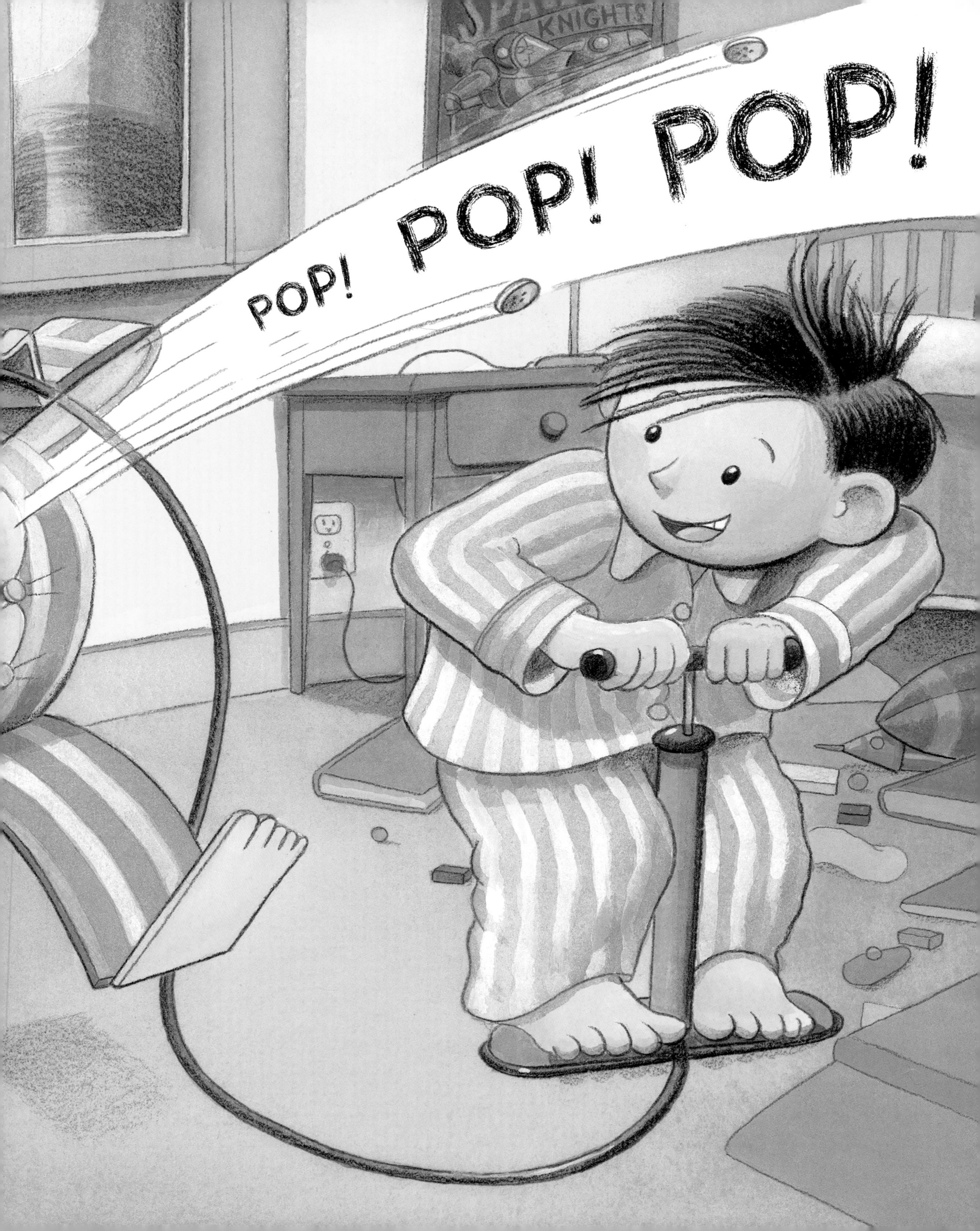
KNIGHTS
POP!
POP!
POP!

Soon he was all rounded out except for his right foot. He shook the foot twice, and it swelled to match the other one. There stood Stanley Lambchop, as if he had never been flat at all.

"Thank you, Arthur," Stanley said. "Thank you very much!"

Mr. and Mrs. Lambchop came in to see what the boys were up to so late at night.

"George!" said Mrs. Lambchop. "Stanley's round again!"

"I'm the one who did it," Arthur said. "I blew him up."

Mrs. Lambchop made hot chocolate to celebrate, and several toasts were drunk to Arthur for his cleverness.

When the little party was over, Mr. and Mrs. Lambchop tucked the brothers back into bed and turned out the light.

"Goodnight," they said.

"Goodnight," said Stanley and Arthur.

Very soon all the Lambchops were asleep.

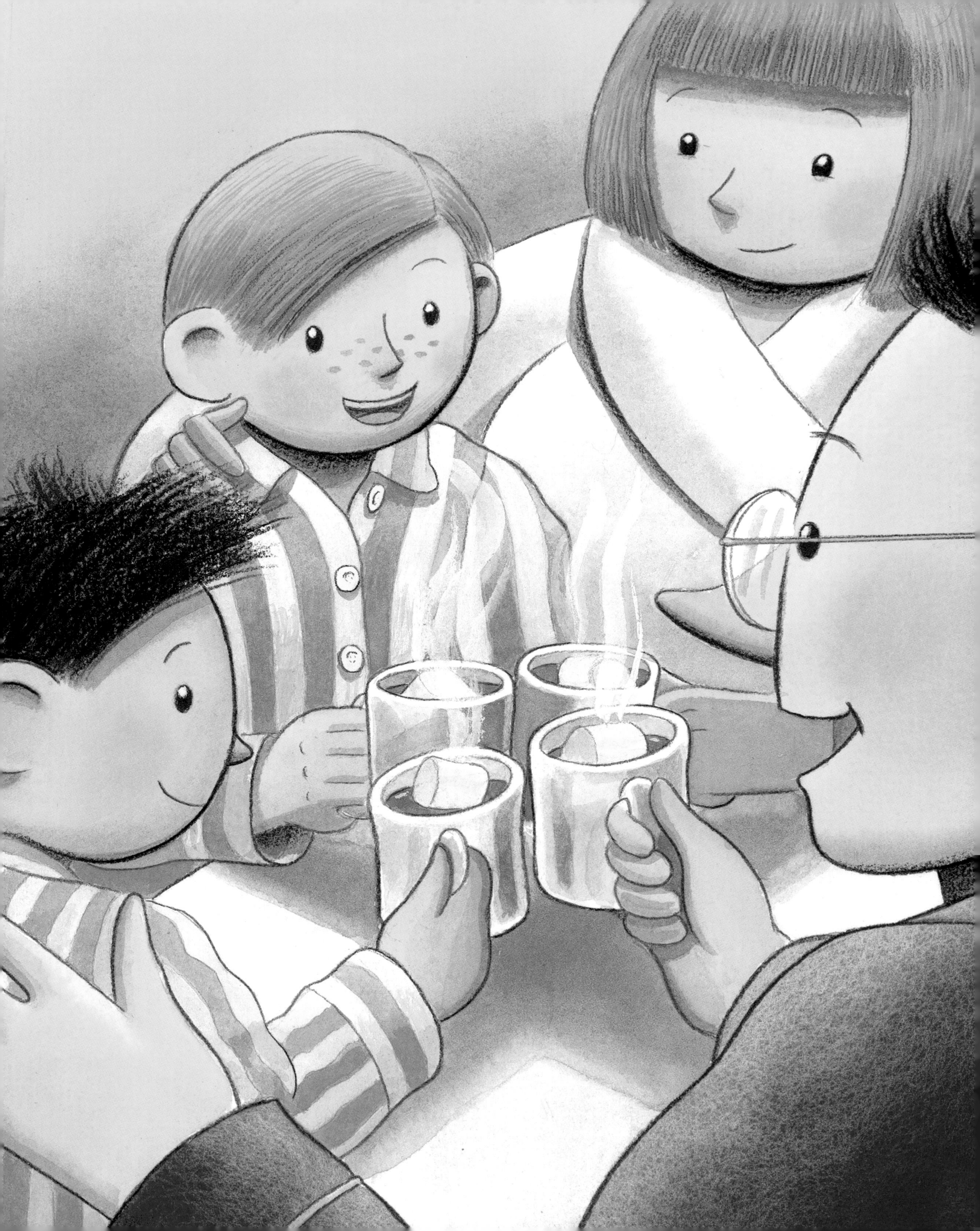

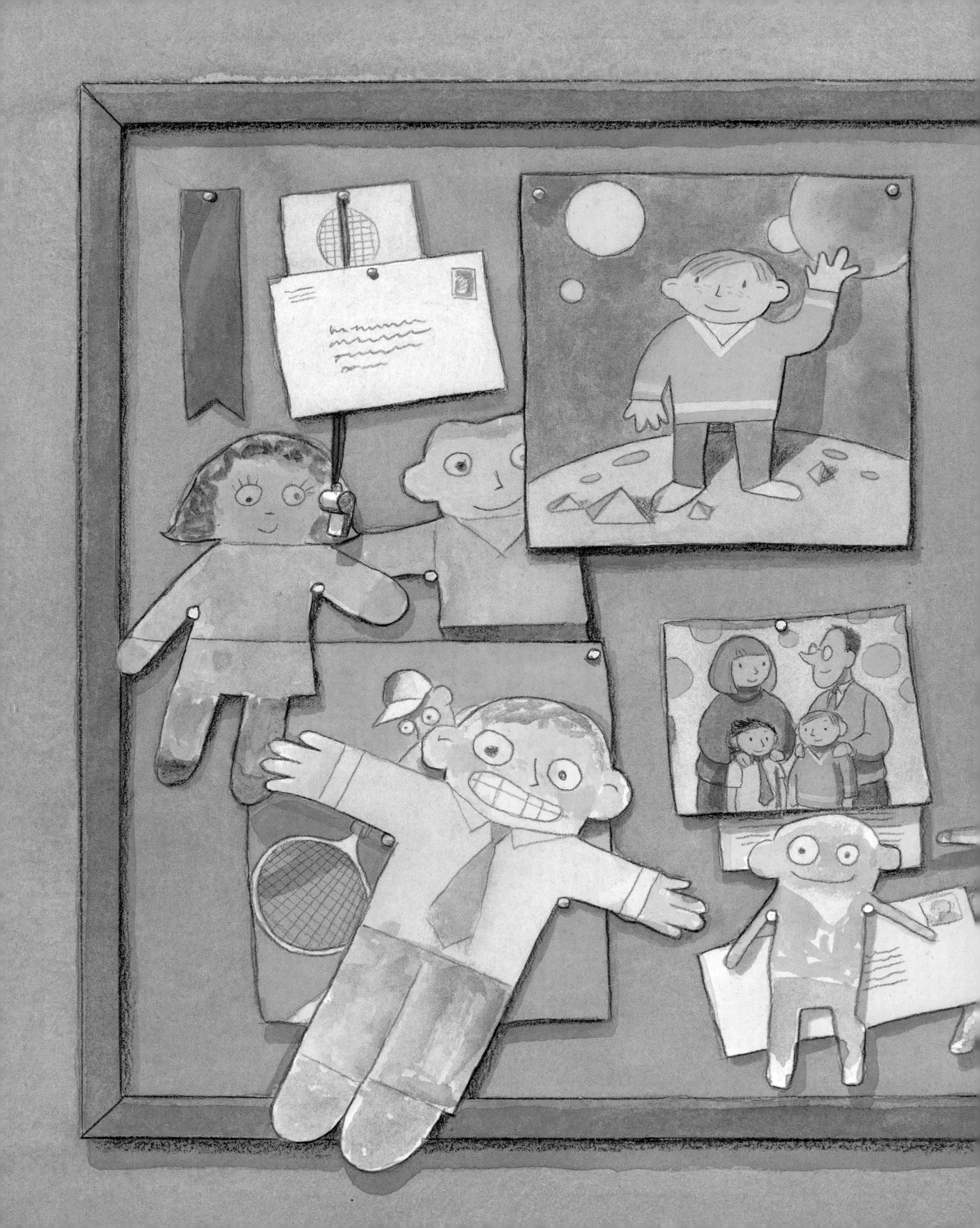